Santa Monica Public Library

I SMP 00 2779825 4

D1446416

SANTA MONICA PUBLIC LIBRARY

JUL – – 2018

Other titles by Kat Meads

For You, Madam Lenin

Not Waving

Senestre on Vacation (as Z.K. Burrus)

Sleep

The Invented Life of Kitty Duncan

Little Pockets of Alarm

When the Dust Finally Settles

*In This Season of Rage and Melancholy Such Irrevocable
        Acts as These*

Sections of this fiction first appeared in *Queen Mob's Tea House.*

Miss Jane:
The Lost Years

Kat Meads

Livingston Press
The University of West Alabama

Copyright © 2018 Kat Meads
All rights reserved, including electronic text
ISBN 13: 978-1-60489-200-0 trade paper
ISBN 13: 978-1-60489-201-7 hardcover
Library of Congress Control Number: 2018932052
ISBN: 1-60489-200-5 trade paper
ISBN: 1-60489-201-3 hardcover
Printed on acid-free paper
Printed in the United States of America by
Publishers Graphics

Hardcover binding by:
Typesetting and page layout: Sarah Coffey
Proofreading: Shelby Parrish, Erin Watt, Tricia Taylor
Cover art: Philip Rosenthal

This is a work of fiction. Any resemblance
to persons living or dead is coincidental.
Livingston Press is part of The University of West Alabama,
and thereby has non-profit status.
Donations are tax-deductible.

first edition

6 5 4 3 3 2 1

Miss Jane:
The Lost Years

Contents

The Quad

1.

What starts, starts somewhere. This the place, the where, Miss Jane encounters a force intent on shaping / re-shaping farm girls, one lucky / unlucky Cracker hick / chick per term. Blank-canvas classroom, second floor, fluorescent lights seizing. A non-emphatic day, a filmy hour, the ninth month of an over-long year is the when. At this conjunction of there / then, as if pre-destined, Miss Jane enters the system, fulfills a quota, succumbs to the mechanics of applied professorial desire. Transmogrifies, one might say, into a standardized course.

How did this happen? How might it not? In any universe actual or invented could our Miss Jane have side-stepped her Lost Years plunge with Prof P? Was what occurred—and will again on these (unsparing) pages—*preventable*? What if Cracker hick / chick Jane had been smarter / dumber, more suspicious / more oblivious, more jaded / more innocent at the cellular level? If, if . . . if only. Alas: our Miss Jane inhabits some of all and most of none of the smart / dumb / suspicious / oblivious / jaded / innocent categories because our Miss Jane is a creature-in-flux, a being in-progress, *not altogether anything quite yet*. As such, she is overly susceptible to calculated ridicule, the readiest of suckers for agendas of improvement pimped by con artists in the shape of higher education despots.

Yes.

Now is as good a time as any to cough up your who-the-hell-cares about Cracker farm girls, to express your gut resistance to yet another academia-sprung tale of power politics, sexual politics, age versus youth, authority's manipulation of head-to-pubes-to-toe confusion. As is your right. Moreover, any assumption regarding an absence of thematic variation: fully justified and totally correct. Thematically we will stay the course. Power politics. Sexual politics. Age versus youth. Authority's manipulation of head-to-pubes-to-toe confusion. The world's themes do not change, why should they here? For variety, look to the ways / means of struggle and resistance, flare-ups of native cunning. No fairy godmothers will appear to offer assistance. Cracker farm girl Jane will be on her own puzzling out the what of this and on her own now travels the muggy, airless hallway of a public university, South Atlantic region, to attend the scheduled class she mistakes for history, not her future. She carries a notebook. She carries a pen. She is wearing a homemade paisley smock with billowing sleeves over sailor jeans. Her face is flushed.

By reason of cloying heat?

The breathless, claustrophobic humidity of the humid South?

Initially.

2.

Settle in, Miss Jane. Familiarize yourself with this site. In flashback it will return—repeatedly. Beige door, beige walls, beige floor, plastic chairs orange as sunset, big, battered, sticky table because seminars require replenishing liquids (coffee, Fresca, Tab) and liquids sometimes / often spill in response to: 1) nervousness, 2) fury. There will be no (heaven forbid) lectures. Only discussion. A civilized discourse in which every voice will be valued, respected, allowed its day and say—except when it won't.

What?!?

You heard correctly.

We will strive not to get sidelined by such an infuriating state of affairs so early on. We will *strive*.

Entering, our Miss Jane smells chalk, sweat (her own, others), an unseen chocolate bar. There is not *quite* enough space around the Department of History seminar table for thirty undergraduates, three graduate teaching assistants and one professor. All will have to wedge. Indoors (in general) Cracker farm girls (in general) fall prey to breath-sucking claustrophobia. But Cracker farm girls are also (in general) polite. If conditions demand, they draw in their elbows. Elbows tucked, Miss Jane selects an orange chair at the table's south corner and, once wedged, breathes shallowly. Another cause for Miss Jane's alarm: the difficulty of taking notes, scrunched, for our Miss Jane, note taker of the highest order, deems anything said by anyone other than herself worthy of record.

Those now assembled are here for the duration of (at least) one class conducted however the fashionably late headliner cares to conduct it. Thirty-three seated women give Prof P's Greek fisherman cap / red beard / turquoise necklace / denim shirt / silver bracelet / faded Levi's / scuffed brogues their rapt attention— or as rapt an attention as can be mustered in a stuffy, windowless classroom on the first day of class, new semester. After TA introductions: the syllabus. Pass it around. Follow along. They will read Chopin, Greer, Millet, Friedan. They will read *Our Bodies Ourselves*. They will be divvied up into four study groups. They will investigate female subjugation, oppression, repression, historical origins and psychological fallout of same. They will write three papers. They will self-grade. They will meet with their assigned mentor once weekly.

Questions?

One.

*Why is a **male** teaching women's history?*

The multi-colored locks of twenty-nine long-haired femmes sweep forward, fifty-eight ears listening hard for the why behind their dick-in-jeans prof. The thirtieth? Distracted by flickering fluorescence, an ache behind the brows, the need to sneak-lick sweat off her upper lip. The room is so very, very *warm*. Comrades on either side sit so very, very *close*. In quest of air, space, a little goddamn breathing room, Miss Jane leans unmistakably backward, breaks the circle, the chain, thereby drawing the unwanted / unnerving counter-attentions of the man in charge, who seizes the opportunity to ask, not answer.

"*Jane*, is it?"

It is.

It is Miss Jane.

4

3.

In the near still-vivid past, moon-faced, freckly TA Alice arrived at a judicious decision: flimsy hair presents best short and feathered, even if such a style accentuates the moony effect. Even if, in muggy season, strands stick and clot around the forehead, cling to temples, negate the more attractive pouf achieved at seven a.m. On the campus of a public university, South Atlantic region, September, late morning, esthetically speaking, TA Alice could use a second hair wash, a reparation impossible to achieve what with classes, what with studying, what with TA-ing. Upshot: on a moment-to-moment basis TA Alice must overcome the dismay of sticky hair to pursue education's higher call.

If you imagine female vanity the single cause of this constant negotiation, your bias is showing. Also (apparently), you have no quarrel with simplistic descriptions. Also: you are definitely not a woman.

From the onset, Miss Jane feels predisposed toward TA Alice. The reason(s): multifarious. Three of Miss Jane's eight aunts are moon-faced; two of the three allowed Miss Jane, playing dress up, to talc their red cheeks white. In Miss Jane's memory, the pleasing scent of talc mingles with "dancing" eyes and merry tunes. Once, strolling campus, Miss Jane happened to stroll behind TA Alice who seemed, with her cap of hair, a she-monk among Victorians. To stand apart in such fashion, Miss Jane interpreted as bravery. Bravery is not a skill Miss Jane takes (or has ever taken) for granted.

Alone with her mentees in the student lounge, TA Alice reveals other laudable attributes: sympathy, empathy, insight, erudition, an egalitarian state of mind.

"We'll collaborate, we'll discover, we'll share findings," says she, thrilling her flock. (Collaboration is a club to which her mentees have not previously been invited.) A prank? A ruse? No, no. No, no. TA Alice is absolutely sincere. TA Alice absolutely believes the times they are a-changin'. In the unfortunate play out of Unfortunate Events to come, it is not TA Alice's ethics that will be called into question. TA Alice's ethics are beside the point.

And why beside the point?

Because TA Alice is operating under three (false) assumptions: 1) that colleagues keep promises; 2) that her mentees will remain her mentees; 3) that there will be no poaching, plucking, or flagrant example of Prof P swinging his big stick and pulling rank on a TA. In consequence, round one of Miss Jane's Series of Unfortunate Events will also deliver a nasty shock to TA Alice, severely testing her baseline optimism and intersexual goodwill.

All very worrying.

All quite discouraging.

For the record: we stand in solidarity with TA Alice. She and her cohorts—without question—are being mistreated by the system and the system's practitioners. But we cannot, *must not*, permit ourselves to become diverted by midnight rallies for union representation, fiery bonfires, fiery speeches, profs and administrators burnt in effigy because we are pledged to stick with Miss Jane's lost-years story and Miss Jane, mere student, wouldn't be invited to TA protests, not even by politically inclusive TA Alice.

4.

This the means by which Miss Jane learns of her hand-off, moon to stick. Between library one and library two: an incline of soil and brick slows the progress of flat-landers the likes of Miss Jane. Between points one and two: Prof P presides, chatting up another long-haired / long-skirted femme, his silver regalia gleaming. Does Miss Jane's inner eye catch sight of that unnatural glint as farm girls on the roam are wont to do? Likely. The problem (one of them): Prof P catches sight of Miss Jane as well. "Jane! A word!" Several words, actually, delivered as fait accompli: Miss Jane's name now resides on Prof P's roster, TA Alice kicked to the curb.

"But," says our Miss Jane.

"She was so...," struggles our Miss Jane.

Feeble as protests go, but Miss Janes are hardly trained to "but" professors. Furthermore: sorrow is often inarticulate. Together they walk the path to Prof P's office, fourth floor, a slog during which Miss Jane's inner eye *should* have noticed a series of pitying / been-there-done-that girls giving *her* the eye. While collecting his mail, Prof P leaves Miss Jane to view his diplomas (Swarthmore, Harvard, Harvard), shelf upon shelf of books taunting Miss Jane's egregious / infinite ignorance and, on what scant wall space remains, artistically blurry images of one girl child, one boy child, ID-ed once Prof P returns as *his* photographs and *his* children (in that order), their birthing agent (lovely Lynette) uncredited.

"And you?"

Her...what? Achievements to date? Miss Jane adopts a

middle distance focus, the better to mentally collate her pitiful few: All-Conference basketball. All-Tournament basketball. 4-H Good Citizen. A gift certificate, once, for selling yearbook ads.

"Scholarship student?" Correct. "First in your family…" Miss Jane waits. Surely Prof P will provide another clue? And so he does, twisting his jewelry, smiling in advance of another poor, unlettered, first-generation college rube's confession. Yes. Miss Jane is the first of her family to matriculate at this public university, South Atlantic region, or at any university in-state or interstellar. Two for two, Prof P is feeling his oats, the satisfaction of his own analytic brilliance. Miss Jane is feeling warm. She would like to open a window. She would like to know whether Prof P's reading list will match TA Alice's reading list because she has already ordered several volumes of the latter, pre-paid with dwindling scholarship funds, and isn't entirely confident that the student store will refund her outlay because an instructor swap is not a situation / dilemma our Miss Jane has previously had to negotiate or underwrite. "Only child?" *Buzz.* With that tell-me demand Prof P's winning streak sputters to a close. Miss Jane is the fifth of five children—a (crowded) biographical fact that (perhaps) explains why Miss Jane is not now hotly offended by Prof P's preening, prying interrogation but rather a tad flattered. For whereas TA Alice was kind, Prof P is *taking a personal interest.*

Indeed he is.

Indeed he is.

5.

And herein the spot where we pretend, for the space of fifteen lines, to give Prof P his propers, allowing for the possibility / entertaining the prospect that Prof P ever so *profoundly* feels a *special, magical, one-of-a-kind, never-to-be-matched* attraction to yet another college gal twelve years his junior. That Miss Jane's lumpen farm girl backwardness delights, refreshes and *salves his tortured soul*. That Miss Jane's eyes or lips or voice or thighs or chin or gait or giggle arouses his prick as if that prick be newly freed from the insufferable prison of *middle age*. That suggestibility, tractability and ease-of-conquest figure nowhere in his selection criteria regarding college gal project number nine, nor do such traits by any means or measure drive and influence Prof P's calculated pursuit of Miss Jane in class and out.

To which we say: *bullshit*. To which we say: *donkey crap*. To which we say: *pig malarkey*. To which we say: *turkey caca*. To which we say: *beetle dung*. To which we say: Hey, Lying Pompous Asshole, we don't give a dump about you or your lying pompous asshole version. On these pages *we* call the shots and your fifteen lines are *done*.

What's that?

You find our stance too polemical, too didactic? Our tone too loud and shrill? Our language too coarse and raunchy? Our manner of expression too bitchily blunt? You'd prefer we find a prettier, more lyrical means of outing the bastard? To you we say: tough titty. Get off the bus. This is *not* your ride. To those still perplexed by the "fuss" over another Cracker hick / chick accepting her hick / chick fate, we here clarify: it's the waste, knuckleheads. The *waste* of *another* hick / chick life.

9

6.

A devotee of outdoor instruction as fashionable alternative to walled-in dialectics, on clear and temperate Monday-Wednesday-Fridays, Prof P can be found declaiming on the quad's lawn. If his "hip" and "witty" declamations draw a larger-than-class-size crowd, so much the better. Further evidence of what he incessantly reminds other faculty and twice (thus far) a community radio audience: "I'm a *very* popular teacher." As appreciative as she is of outdoor versus indoor instruction, Miss Jane misses TA Alice. She misses her (previously assigned) study group. In the quad, per the syllabus, Prof P discourses on Chopin, Greer, Millet, Friedan and (bonus) Steinem as Miss Jane listens, taking careful notes before Prof P snatches her notebook and lobs it elsewhere, knuckle-grazing her crotch in the process.

"Don't scribble. *Think.*"

Is Miss Jane incensed by the interruption? Flabbergasted by the temerity? Does the notebook-less Jane feel violated body and mind? None of the above. Miss Jane's sole response is wild, breath-sucking, belly-shrinking panic. To remember *anything* Miss Jane *must* write that anything down—and now she *can't*. Apart, offside, unclaimed, Miss Jane's writing pad remains where any campus dog might sniff it, shit it or chew it to bits while our Miss Jane, every inch and atom of her jonesing for the tossed, moves not a muscle to retrieve it.

A foretaste of inactions to come?

Sadly, yes.

7.

A fall season that feels spring-ish, a quad littered with the lollying. And where be our Miss Jane? Seated beside lollying Prof P, a young miss summoned to the quad on a non-class day for additional one-on-one edification. We know this because we know this; the campus community will know this tomorrow because a roaming *Daily TarBelly* photog captures their duo, Miss Jane all hair, Prof P propped on his motor scooter helmet, bald spot exposed, hand edging toward Miss Jane's thigh.

As much as we appreciate the scenic incongruities, as much as we applaud the thick-haired photog's snarky dis of roué Prof P, as much as we respect tight deadlines and photojournalism's truth-telling mandate, we wish the *Daily TarBelly* editor-in-chief had passed on immortalizing this particular image. Friday's edition put to bed, printed and dispersed, Miss Jane is…chagrined. Her journalism-major roomie Cinda G is apoplectic, a whirling spitball of accusation and reprimand. Flapping damning newsprint, Cinda G lays into Miss Jane like nobody's business.

What the hell is going on, Jane?!?

Ah.

If Miss Jane *knew*, if Miss Jane could *say*, how much less a confusing mishmash of power to the people and dictatorial practice her semester would be.

8.

But, wait: is there no honey nearer Miss Jane's *age* in the picture / in the wings?

Kinda, sorta, in a manner of speaking.

And would that "manner" cover screwing?

On occasion.

Impossibly complex or impossibly simple, Seth B and Miss Jane's relationship. Each would rather forfeit a nose, lick a cactus, die a tumorous death than "tie the other down" (in the non-bedroom application) or "stand in the other's way" in terms of dreams, schemes and destinies. Neither cares to select movie or menu for two because, as Calvinist seedlings, each considers presumption the deadliest of sins. Given the bulldozer brutalities of the universe, in principle this attitude may appear refreshing. In situ, the results are: repetitive swallowing and conversational dead air. Regularly the last in line at Arby's, Seth B and Miss Jane approach the closing clerk in a state of sheepish apology. But they've got to eat: they're starving. Holding back is grueling exercise.

With each the other: shy as jellyfish, tender as bean sprouts, mute as mimes. Happy (happiest?) is our Miss Jane perched on a stool, reading, Seth B crankshaft tinkering, his motorcycle (not scooter) the hand-me-down of an uncle gone to un-presumptive glory. Seth B and Miss Jane in the sack? Pretty compatible there too, for there tentativeness gets KO-ed by need, greed, that selfish motherfucker desire, pleasure achieved in wordless motion. Another pleasure: the voiceless sequel. On Seth B's bike, Miss Jane holding tight, a ride-about in ebon night on country roads, mist in the trees, gnats in their ears, a million zillion pulsing stars, speed for the sake of speed, and our Miss Jane unafraid.

9.

Not a scholarship student but programmed by nurture and nature for thrift, Miss Jane's roomie Cinda G arrived at her educational home-away-from-home carting a hot plate, a month's worth of Pop Tarts and five cases of chicken soup. Cinda G believes—and let no outsider *presume* otherwise—that she achieves her best critical thinking stirring her nightly gumbo. Closed-circuit dynamics. Problem(s) surrounded, encapsulated, solved.

Across from Cinda G's clang and bang prep, Miss Jane crunches Saltines—the only sustenance her tummy has accepted without retaliation for more than a week. Cracker crumbs on her knees, cracker crumbs on the sheets, cracker crumbs for the dorm mice that rely on distracted undergrads for bounty. Notwithstanding a severe shortage of saliva, Miss Jane has just (again) explained to Cinda G, who has just (again) let loose an "easy lay / easy A" diatribe, that her women's history course is a self-graded course. In turn, Cinda G (heatedly) argues: grades are grades; transcripts, transcripts, and only *profs* record grades.

Time out.

Miss Jane chews; Cinda G stirs. The windows of 214 Harker Dorm steam up. Despite (mounting) evidence to the contrary, Cinda G *is* on Miss Jane's side. Peering deep into her cauldron, she floats this solution: "Drop the course. Get out of it that way." Good idea, but non-implementable. Miss Jane's already checked. To drop a course without adding another jeopardizes her scholarship funds. Catch 22: the add-a-course dates have passed. That Miss Jane has investigated the drop option we take as the first (encouraging) sign that, in the deepest interior of her warring Cracker self, a grievance has sprouted. Cracker grievances (in general) start small, chub up and once in play enjoy the half-life of a plutonium isotope. They can (also) stew, simmer and boil up like chicken soup, which brings us back round to Cinda G and her second solution: "Ask the TA to take you back." Since Miss Jane's chewing slows to the rate of a masticating cow—fair assumption—she's giving Cinda G's alternate a mental once-over.

And why not?

It's an askin' world.

10.

Family tradition, thereby Miss Jane tradition: avoid confrontation at all costs. In defensive mode, if hectored, fall silent; abstain from contradicting or by any further means engaging / enraging the accuser. Seek no additional clarification for the (supposed) wrong you've committed. Wait it out. If personally compromised by a fit of hysterical weeping brought on by irregular menses, menopausal hormones, a bad fishing day, take to the fields. Shriek-weep to an audience of ditch turtles and curious crows. If the yen to tear someone a new one persists, walk it off. *Keep walking* until recomposed into a neutral being disinclined to disrupt household serenity / mores.

In theory, Miss Jane's conversation with TA Alice should not classify as confrontation. From Miss Jane's perspective—first, last and middle—hers is a heartfelt plea. From TA Alice's perspective: ambush; a reminder of the powerlessness of a TA to undo damage(s) done. In such a state, how will TA Alice (wherever waylaid) give equitable hearing to our Miss Jane? Earliest clues the stairwell encounter will not go our gal's way: TA Alice's initial startle, followed by a concerted effort *not* to finger-fork her hair.

TA Alice! Just call the shit a shit and be done with it! No one, least of all Miss Jane, will blame *you*. Instead, TA Alice remains distressingly silent, one foot on one stair, the other on another. Minutes pile up. Excruciatingly sensitive to the accumulation, Miss Jane realizes she's using up TA Alice's break to ask for what is essentially a favor. (Incorrect. What Miss Jane is asking for is a TA insurrection.) Asking to rejoin TA Alice's group, Miss Jane has a tough time refraining from latching onto TA Alice's ankle / arm / neck in lifeline fashion. For her part, TA Alice has a tough time explaining a policy that allows neither undergraduates to choose their mentors nor graduate mentors to choose their mentees. The nub of it: TA Alice can't authorize Miss Jane's shift-back because she's (merely) TA Alice.

But, whoa!

Check out our Miss Jane, screwing up her courage for another go. Peony red, panting like a heifer, she asks: "Then can I sit-in?" What to do, what to do, TA Alice? With whom will you align: the lower orders or the upper? "I'm afraid that wouldn't be fair." *Fair?!?* Did TA Alice just imply Miss Jane wrangles for double access off a single tuition? (Brilliant dodge, if so. No Cracker farm child would dream of demanding more than her share.)

And that, sister femmes, is that.

The lifeboat carrying TA Alice shoves off, leaving our Miss Jane alone in choppy waters. "I'm sorry, Jane," TA Alice calls, disappearing into bureaucratic fog (i.e., the TA lounge). "I wish I could have helped."

Our Miss Jane wishes the same.

11.

Surely Miss Jane has other courses, other professors, to counterbalance, if not countervail, the lecherous attentions of Prof P?

Three in the running.

First and foremost: famous, formidable, feminist poet Carolyn Z—the envy of English Department colleagues on multiple levels, *deeply* resented for her one-course-per-semester teaching load and bulging Rolodex. In Carolyn Z's majestic Colonial Revival, two blocks from campus, on every table and window ledge: gushingly signed editions from every published poet in America alongside chatty notes from Bella A, Shirley C and Geraldine F. Tall, regal Carolyn Z is genetically blessed with (or cultivates) the kind of take-no-prisoners voice that paralyzes deans as well as undergraduates. Spectacularly fierce, she will not be put off, condescended to or trifled with by the patriarchy in charge. Miss Jane *worships* Carolyn Z. In The Magnificent's classroom, Miss Jane struggles to contain her jaw-drop awe; she also struggles to translate Borges's "Calle Desconocida." If Carolyn Z instructed Miss Jane to shave her head, as an act of respect and homage Miss Jane would—at the very least—chop herself some bangs. But rarely, rarely is Carolyn Z moved to instruct; she prefers to lead by example, an example (to be brutally honest) far above the attainment levels of our Miss Jane.

Next candidate? Documentarian Hernandez, who snags a pirated edition of "American Family" and tosses his semester plan to accommodate a twelve-episode screening. Question: can any viewer view Pat Loud in her gilded cage and miss the caged part? Statistically improbable, but there *are* mitigating factors. The RTVMP projector is temperamental; the classroom's shades inadequate. Light leaks in, bleaching the Santa Barbarians' year-round tans as well as Pat's corneas, significantly diminishing the effect of their caged / crazed alarm. Also distracting from the Perils of Pat: pink fuchsia, purple ceanothus, roseate oleander, Santa Ynez chaparral, Santa Ynez sage, the wide blue Pacific, spiky palms that clatter, the utter absence of biting varmints whenever Pat chain-smokes poolside, staring into another answerless night.

Miss Jane's last chance: Dr. Miner, psych nerd / Skinnerite who loathes teaching but can't figure out how else to remain solvent. Delivered from a folding chair, Dr. Miner's lectures start and stop precisely on time. Operant conditioning, positive and negative reenforcement, behavior the technology. Legs crossed, arms crossed, Dr. Miner talks not at his students but at the ceiling, reminding Miss Jane of her dear, dear Uncle Keith who eschewed eye contact in favor of…eschewing. Pertinent info to keep in mind when assessing Miss Jane's behaviorist receptivity: although her family tree sags with tent preachers, never, never has it germinated a *Free Will* Baptist, determinism no way / no how a new or shocking concept. Be that as it may, note these scored passages in Miss Jane's cherished *Beyond Freedom and Dignity*:

> Who is to construct the controlling environment and to what end?

> Almost all living things act to free themselves from harmful contacts.

Hmm, we say. Hmm.

In Dr. Miner's course, Miss Jane's (non-self-graded) A's roll in, her weekly papers evaluated by a TA who, under

Dr. Miner's tutelage, doesn't know or care whom he's grading. Miss Jane, we notice, has begun to keep her B.F. tome close, much as her tent preacher ancestors hugged their King Jameses. Nowhere near the quad is Miss Jane when Prof P finds her, vigorously underlining. You're assuming Prof P scoffs, scolds, tosses the hardback as he did the notebook? Nope. "May I borrow it?" As Miss Jane mistakes go, handing over her Skinner to a vehement self-actualist isn't the worst goof. But it's not good. It's definitely not good. Those bracketed paragraphs, those margin notes, those question marks, those exclamation points? Diary, more or less. And now Prof P has access.

12.

As (near daily) confirmed by Prof P, Miss Jane is woefully under-read in every discipline. Any book she sits down with in the library stacks counts / should count as a blow against the chokehold of her cultural illiteracy. But where to enter a forest many thousand volumes wide and thick? Deprived of her Skinner, Miss Jane's Dewey Decimal hot spot migrates. Turning her back on psych's pseudo-science, she wanders toward the home of pseudonyms, existence explained / dramatized by professional liars. In the under-illuminated, non-fumigated lit-sy enclave she seeks out an empty carrel, resolves to ignore the odors of book mold, crusty socks and rodent poop. Some occupant before her has scratched "putrid," "please" and "punt" on the carrel's lone shelf—the sort of tantalizing riddle that makes our Miss Jane feel unbearably stupid, followed closely by unbearably adrift. As best she can she breathes through her mouth, ignores the slapping footfalls of who knows whom, sticks to her autodidact agenda. First up, other Janes: Austen, Bowles, Crazy J and Eyre. Skip the land of make-believe and there'd be the legacies of Addams, Seymour, Pierce and Goodall to peruse. But our Miss Jane is where she is. The 800s.

Because we see what Miss Jane can't, we see the fellow, zipper down, skulking among the 830s—also the body part he's fondling. As resident exhibitionist, he's got a lot of territory to prowl but prefers a Teutonic launch pad. In the murkiness, Miss Jane at first fails to connect tumid pink with wanking equipment. When she does, she and her bundle of Janes beeline it to the brightly lit glass-domed reading room where no sickos (freelance or salaried) can sneak up and surprise her.

She reads:

Emma Woodhouse, handsome, clever, and rich, with a comfortable home and happy disposition seemed to unite some of the best blessings of existence; and had lived nearly twenty-one years in the world with very little to distress or vex her.

—a passage that causes our not rich / not handsome / Cracker-disposition-ed striver to heave a sigh, gaze drifting.

No sense pretending.

No sense denying.

No sense pussyfooting around it.

The acquisition of knowledge presents—and shall present—a vexing challenge for our Miss Jane. (No fairy godmothers among cast and crew, remember?)

13.

Following date night with Seth B, Miss Jane sleeps in, cutting two classes, blowing off her mentee appointment with Prof P. For brunch she snacks on mini-Snickers. Early afternoon she rearranges books, minutely inspects her hair, trims split ends. Early evening, wearing the same yeasty pj's, she returns to bed, coughs, chokes, hacks up phlegm. At midnight she wakes to Cinda G's hunt and peck, a scratchy throat, incipient fever. Nailing it, first go, Cinda G declares: "You're sick. No offense but keep to your half of the room. I'm on deadline." (Cinda G is actually working on an English paper tangentially related to the Reformation but practices reporter jargon at every opportunity to bolster the habit.)

In the bathroom, peeing, Miss Jane feels decidedly woozy. Wiping, she keeps one hand on the stall's coolest tiles. Nodding off, she dreams. Not a toilet dream, not even a water dream. Farm girl on the stroll, she passes Great Aunt Sylvie's ivy-covered house and spies the basketball team captain in an upper-story window. "Not going back to school," declares that mirage. "Staying here to recuperate." What startles Awake Jane is Dream Jane's reply: "I recuperated here too." Because: 1) Great Aunt Sylvie detested teenagers (the "scourge of God") and would never have allowed one, related or random, inside her house; and 2) because Great Aunt Sylvie detested ivy ("no better than a weed") and would never have allowed its tendrils to deface her home.

As soon as Seth B hears from Cinda G that Miss Jane's ailing, he drops his motorcycle wrench to make an Arby's run. Cinda G won't venture close enough to the pair to share roast beef and fries but Seth B, unafraid of contagion, nestles in alongside Miss Jane in her sickwear. Propped against Seth B's shoulder, Miss Jane chews, swallows, digests, feels better but fails to recognize that she *always* feels better alongside Seth B, whatever her body temp. To improve Miss Jane's spirits, Seth B not only brings grub, he brings *For the Roses*. To get to the Record Bar before every copy sold, Seth B had to (also) skip class. "Joni!" Cinda G squeals and fires up the lava lamp. In mute reverence the three listen to the LP straight through, both sides, four times. *Learning / peaceful / good dog / trees.* Much as we'd love to report (or imply) that a groggy, Joni-inspired Jane fantasized escape to British Columbia or some other Canadian / Grecian / Australian outpost, that claim would constitute false reporting and as such terrifically offend Cinda G, whom we have no inclination to offend. (Cinda G called in Seth B, after all.) Also: Miss Jane is not a rock star with rock star travel funds; she's a *scholarship student*. She's going nowhere, especially not tonight, fever one hundred one and holding, nose still plenty snotty. In less time than it takes to sneeze she's fast asleep, Seth B her pillow, Dorm Mother R having blown off her final boys-out inspection to watch *The Tonight Show* starring Debbie Reynolds.

Altogether, a blow-it-off cabal.

14.

Miss Jane (still peaked) and Seth B (still rumpled) drink sodas, munch toast in the a.m. dining hall. Carbonation is essential. Sugar is essential. Carbonation and sugar in gallon combinations have gotten Miss Jane through many a dreaded day and will perform a similar service throughout her Lost Years (aka Dread Future). Nevertheless, carbonated sugar cannot foment miracles. Should she make it to Ancient History, 8 a.m., Miss Jane will (again), mind drifting, confuse the Greeks with the Romans. In Spanish lab / section C, Seth B will (again) bungle subjunctive mood, unable to master a third language having yet to master the crucial second: standard English (the plight of many a Cracker).

For a half-beat longer than usual this morning Miss Jane's goodbye hug fails to release. Seth B notices, his pleasure compromised by concern. Maybe Miss Jane isn't up to the task of class? Maybe she should go back to bed? *Can't. Too far behind. Was behind before. Now: Very. Far. Behind.* Seth B nods. What must be endured must be. Miss Jane has every intention—*every intention*—of subjecting herself to in-class interiors before fate throws up a much more appealing setting and seat: a deserted, open-air bench. Upon that splintery plank she plops, doing nothing, a lovely drifty nothing, until a certain prof-on-the-prowl catches her in the act. Does Miss Jane plead lingering ill health for her malingering, the bodily need to breathe where she breathes? She does not. She splotches: a student caught slacking off by a professor. "Appalled" by such "unconscionable dawdling," Prof P "congratulates" our Miss Jane for "living up to her amateur self." When at last the hectoring expert departs, still splotchy Jane opens a new blue notebook to doodle this:

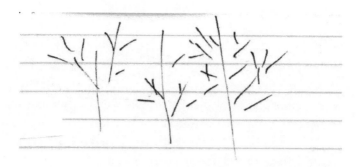

Which turns into this:

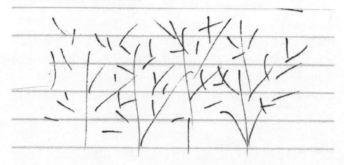

Which turns into this:

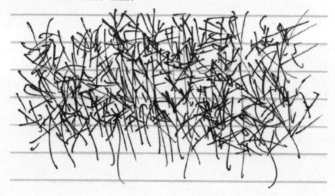

Because doodling *used to* help amateur Jane see the forest for the trees.

15.

Headed to Cinda G's summer internship interview—
though the season be barely fall—Cinda G drives; Miss
Jane rides. (Two-hour trip each way.) Cinda G suffers no
"unconscionable" lethargy; Cinda G's genetically me-
ga-dosed with *get-up-and-go*. Between Cinda G's toes, *no
grass grows*. Accordingly, relaxation plays no part in any
road experience with Cinda G. To meet the challenges
of traveling faster A to B and besting the beast known
as traffic, Cinda G adopts a two-pronged strategy: out-
maneuver, outrun. Although difficult for Miss Jane to
maintain her dreamy state in a car piloted by Cinda G,
she likes the look of an empty roadway as much as (if
not more than) her eliminate-the-competition roomie
and is therefore willing to tuck and roll with the curves.
Because Cinda G is a multitasker, she can navigate as
well as yap. After mentally tallying her to-dos: 1) wow interviewer, 2) hunt for an apartment, 3) shop for business
attire, she's open to other topics, including what Miss
Jane's lined up for the summer.

Lined up? For *next* summer?

Miss Jane hasn't thought. Probably "the usual": creek
fishing with Dad. Beachcombing with Mom. Water-
skiing with cousins. Chopping weeds. Mowing grass.
Thinning the strawberry patch. Sweet corn. Sweet tea.
Morning glories. Yellow flies. Crickets. Slicing to bits any
stray viper that slithers across her path… "Seth doing
his usual too?" Cinda G interrupts, requiring Miss Jane
to shift reveries to Seth B, on-site mechanic at his aunt's
garage, six counties removed from swamps / swamp vi-
pers and Miss Jane's family farm. "Is that a yes?" Cinda
G confirms.

Probably.

Miss Jane hasn't thought.

16.

Almost there, the gals spot radio towers. Arrived, they stare at pocked cinder blocks, crumbling steps and peeling roof shingles. To those unpromising loci, Cinda G reacts with *grim determination*. Shithole or no, she needs three months of broadcast training and by the power invested in her she's going to get it, *no matter what*. In the lobby's single chair, to prevent shading Cinda G's chances (because there *are* employers known to judge by the company one keeps), Miss Jane makes a point of smiling indiscriminately at all objects, animate and in-, moving and still. Deprived of Cinda G chat, Miss Jane must rely on the diversions of spider webs, dust bunnies, finger whorls on glass. But can even our Miss Jane remain *wholly* diverted for one hour twenty-three minutes by arachnids, dust, ghost prints and indiscriminate grinning? She cannot. (Though, hey! **A** for effort.) At minute forty-eight: a moment of noncommittal drift. At minute forty-nine: another of same. After which, Miss Jane's brain revives the speed-along conversation containing the roadblock question *what cha gonna do*, followed by lobby-chair reflections about the aimless trajectory of her summer / life.

Oh dear.

Oh my.

If confused by our less than jubilant response, we remind you of Miss Jane's origins / origin story. Born of a fatalistic tribe enslaved by drought and hurricane scenarios, dependent on the vicissitudes of earth and sky, Crackers are ace brooders. Once started, a Cracker hick / chick will brood to beat the band, brooding her raison d'être, an atavistic predilection, a fallback trope. So, no: we don't consider brooding, per se, progress. To brood is not to act; it is to brood.

17.

Broods, once begun, soak a being. Drippy, our Miss Jane. Drippy and drear. And thus we caution—no, implore!—that you bear in mind the drippy dreariness manifest in this college senior, the deep blue state of her heart / body / soul, as you judge the icky, tacky, cliché-ridden sequence that follows.

In prep, a recap. She: farm-bred Cracker chick, under-schooled in books and life, overly susceptible to ridicule. He: divorced father of two under ten, twelve years her senior, tenured, salaried, summers free to "perfect his photographic eye," bald spot covered by Greek fisherman's cap, the remainder of him hiding in plain sight (i.e., teaching).

Once before Miss Jane entered Prof P's bach pad. The occasion: an after-reading event. Inexplicably, the poet of vengeful poems dedicated to betrayer men "in hopes they fall off their motorcycles and break their necks" was *not* introduced to the campus audience by the magnificent Carolyn Z; rather, by Prof P. During Prof P's stagey intro, the poet of vengeful motorcycle poems peered at her introducer as at a species extinct. At the podium herself, the poet kicked off her set with: *stay silent / keep away from sharks*. Did Miss Jane, eighth row, fourth seat in, decode the warning? Contractually obliged to party with students thereafter, the poet of vengeful motorcycle poems settled on Prof P's dinette chair, drank tepid beer, signed books and wished (we surmise) she'd never left California. Pestered to sign her host's copy of her book, she scribbled "No surprise" above her initials. Again, Miss Jane, again! *Heed the poets!*

A matter of pride, Prof P's bach pad—first floor apartment, scuzzy side street. A matter of principle,

Prof P's residence "among the workers" (or the collegiate equivalent): busboys, office temps, library book shelvers. Inside décor: candle-dripped Chianti bottles, jazz LPs, perpetually unmade bed. It is to this cave our Miss Jane returns, semester winding down, to "discuss her final grade." Optimal outcome(s): Miss Jane argues her (promised) self-grading rights; Miss Jane protests a broken contract; Miss Jane reports Prof P's self-grading sham to his dean. (There are no optimal outcomes.) "Hanging out with me doesn't mean you get a bye on assignments." (When has Miss Jane assumed / presumed she got a "bye" on anything?) "You still owe me a paper." (In fact, she doesn't; she turned in the paper weeks ago.) Bamboozle the prey is a tactic that has worked before for Prof P and works now again. Confused, alarmed, disconsolate, mortified, our Miss Jane. "But I did turn it in!" Will she, because of the mysteriously missing, fail the course? Will Prof P allow her to "make up" the work? Does she have time to replicate what she's already written? Will Prof P *accept* a make-up / replication / rewrite???

Cue the consoler.

For those still inclined to give Prof P the benefit of the doubt (e.g., *He collects scads of papers! Miss Jane's might have blown from his motor scooter sack!*): SOD OFF. You're of absolutely no use to our Miss Jane who, from here on out, needs all the (non-Prof P) help she can assemble.

In consoling mode, Prof P's hands drift. "Wow," exclaims Primo Bastard. "Hugh ass."

Last question, final exam. Miss Jane sleeps with her professor: a) because she's down a paper; b) because she's in the grip of a drippy / drear malaise; c) in apology for her ignorance; d) in apology for her broad Cracker ass; e) because she's been played by a middle-aged hippie poseur who should be FUCKING ASHAMED of his FUCKING MANIPULATIVE SELF.

Correct answer: all of the above.

18.

From Prof P's bach apartment into the night our Miss Jane carries her disparaged ass and stunned heart. If we could pretty this up ("accompanied by nightingale song," "bathed in the fragrance of clematis," "marveling at heavens bright"), we would. But it stinks of urine outside Prof P's pad and Miss Jane isn't gazing skyward, isn't altogether conscious a sky exists, star-bright or cloud-blotchy. For all intents and purposes Miss Jane could be in a vault undersea. She's processing not a whit of the outer world, locked in her inner-in-ner. And just now? It ain't pretty inside Miss Jane's in-ner-inner. It's a dank dark sinkhole of sucking doubt.

Conclusions from which our Miss Jane longed to snatch comfort: 1) what just happened would never happen again; 2) Prof P would be as abashed as she, should their paths hereafter intersect; 3) Prof P's ap-praisal of her ass did *not* constitute an attack on her lineage and gene pool; 4) Prof P did *not* equate a big ass with failure of character (i.e., discipline). Salient point missed? Awfulness of the copulation. Even if Prof P had been a lad of twenty-two, they would have made a crummy couple coupling. Miss Jane's and Prof P's bods don't jibe (and never will).

Oops. We didn't mean to reveal that nail in the coffin quite so soon—but: what the hey. Secret's out. So here we state without equivocation: in the sack, Miss Jane needs no instruction. Knows what she wants when she wants it and how she wants it done. Nurses no confu-sions about the specifics of what pumps her blood / swells her clit / brings home pleasure in thrilling cre-scendo and achieves it, thank you very much, with the compatible *without fail.*

The dorm room door scrapes. Cinda G wakes. "Seth called. I told him you were in the library." Credit to Cinda G for that tight-spot lie, but: even a professorially unentangled Miss Jane cramming for finals would never linger in the library after midnight. Farm girls believe in sleep. Cherish sleep. View sleep as the cure-all for (almost) all that ails. And. Um. Seth B knows his farm girls inside out and sideways.

19.

Finals over, semester done, in borrowed truck versus usual transport, Seth B drives Miss Jane home for the holidays, the latter still suffering congested mornings / achy evenings, still "under the weather"—or so they both agree to label the primary cause of Miss Jane's disquiet. Even in bracing December, Seth B's motorcycle would have been the better choice, open-throttle noise their mile-after-mile no-talk excuse. *This* silence is of their own making: Miss Jane concussed with confusion(s); Seth B wordlessly aggrieved. To remind: Crackers do not **discuss** dilemmas. The unsaid, they axiomatically assume, remains unsaid *for a reason*.

At the farm, Miss Jane's parents hug it out with Seth B, invite him to overnight on the couch. After a bacon and corned beef breakfast, Seth B and Miss Jane trek the land, accompanied by family dogs and one adventurous cat. In a clearing of maple trees, they lean together, united in admiration of winter's strip to basics: bark and limb and twig and root. "I'm…" says Miss Jane, swallows.

What, Miss Jane, *what?*

Say it! Use your words!

Unburden yourself!

Share with the noble Seth B what you're thinking, feeling, wanting, needing…

Nope.

Not gonna happen.

20.

For a glorious two weeks our Miss Jane manages to forget the existence of her public university, South Atlantic region, along with the menace there employed. Presents to wrap, cakes to bake. A pine Christmas tree to cut and tote through the woods with Daddy. On Christmas eve, masses of family squeeze in, doubling up as need be, hanging off chair arms, squatting on the floor, one bathroom for the bunch and not a soul complaining. Miss Jane's be-aproned mom and aunts coordinate with the speed of short order cooks, turkey, ham, sweet potatoes, butter biscuits, Lima beans, the full complement piled onto plates that have been pooled from the cupboards of five kitchens. To drink: eight pitchers of sweet tea lined up on the washing machine. They eat in shifts, have to, appetites / laughter hearty. Dishes washed, leftovers divided, women join the living room crush; kids sneak in the dogs. A puppy pees on wrapping paper—but only pees. No one knocks over the tree. Goodnights exchanged, Miss Jane's mom discovers a serving dish not hers. No matter. Tomorrow at Grandma's house, they'll do it all again.

Beclouding this idyll? A December 27 confluence of improbables: 1) Cinda G postpones her final "books" semester to replace a broadcast intern who quit without notice; 2) Prof P places a call. First try, he gets a busy signal, Cinda G just then conveying plans and apologies to a dumbfounded Jane. "I know this leaves you in a pickle, roommate-wise." In the wake of such news, Miss Jane staggers off, leaving her closer-to-the-phone mom to pick up Prof P's redial. "Jane? Hon? Your professor? Calling???" High-voltage alarm passes mom to daughter and back again. This crossing-of-castes communication? Something's not *right*. But the wrong that

Miss Jane's mama fears (failed grade, lost scholarship) isn't correct either. Mom and daughter's dual anxieties snap and pop, rousing the critters. Four pups congregate on the back steps to quiver and whine. "Hello?" Miss Jane whispers into a black receiver still warm from her last prolonged clutching. "The runaway," Prof P jeers, causing Miss Jane's cheeks to flame in a drafty Cracker house, late December. Mom, maintaining a discreet distance, worries her dishrag; Miss Jane worries the phone cord. "And now the deaf and dumb act. Pathetic." Pathetically in over her head is what Miss Jane feels—as well as (pay attention, Jane!): trapped, cornered, forced. "I expected better." Click.

Bishop Street

1.

Cinda G in absentia, new-semester funk engulfing, option-deprived Miss Jane accepts (bloody hell!) Prof P's proposition to bunk with him at his new rental: a house on Bishop Street. Listen: just because we despise the guy doesn't mean we discount his box-in / shame the vic / bully-boy prowess. But why would a coercion ninja waste time and talents on the likes of Miss Jane? She who fails to appreciate the specialness of the "care" visited upon her? She who fled his (previous) digs without a word? She of the ass size not to his liking? Why here / now does Prof P push the conquest agenda to cohabit stage?

Puzzler, yeah?

Speculatively / ideologically / psychically opposed to dwelling on Prof P's side of the fence for more than a nonce, we've given the matter some—as opposed to extensive—thought. Among the possibilities: *most* women (Miss Jane excluded) have, at this stage of creation, learned to steer clear of free-range Prof Pees and associate wannabes. Related: Prof P and his ilk are no longer the beneficiaries of limitless quarry because how many Miss Janes *still exist* (in public universities, South Atlantic region or elsewhere) to be literally and figuratively dicked with? Fond as we are of explanations one and two, we suspect the reason with legs is this: after years of quick-time success, quick-time success has begun to bore Prof P. Enter Cracker Jane, an undergrad he mounts (in the sexual sense) but whose Cracker nature he cannot immediately *sur*mount, thereby presenting a novelty, a challenge, a change.

Makes sense, yeah?

But enough about the dicker. How fares our Miss Jane on the threshold of assuming a Bishop Street address? Dazed. Disoriented. *Dangerously* drifty (aka a muzzy mess). Since we can't warn the Cracker hick / chick poised to become Prof P's in-house lab rat, we warn you. In this chunk of Unfortunate Events, a shit-storm of nastiness brews and breaks. There will be siege. There will be torment. There will be *major* distress. Small, medium and massive humiliation(s) will be visited on our Miss Jane, her self-preservation severely tested. Mind games of an increasingly devious sort will be played. Incidents of intimidation will escalate. Strong-arm displays of might and moxie will proliferate. Force (of various sort) will be exerted. Unfair advantage will (again) be taken. Guilt, the whipping stick, will (again) be brandished and applied. Ultimately at stake: Miss Jane's guarded / close-mouthed / disinclined to feelings-share disposition. For Bishop Street is the place, the where, Prof P mounts a protracted assault on Cracker Reserve. The pretext? Enlightenment, mon cher. "To Discuss Is to Learn."

2.

In case our (belabored) point missed its mark: with Miss Jane nightly in his bed, Prof P's mission grows exponentially more ambitious. To subdue a body, one thing; to reprogram a mind, a thing far grander. In the name of acculturation—the substitution of his culture for hers—Prof P intends to fuck (further) with Miss Jane's mind.

Dorm rat prior to lab rat, Miss Jane's contribution to household furnishings is a suitcase stuffed with paisley smocks and jeans. Prof P's last apartment rented furnished. If the two are to have a stool to sit on, a lamp to read by, acquisitions are required. (Already on-site, two exceptions: Prof P's walnut desk and desk chair, assigned and occupying a room of their own.) Miss Jane holds nothing against the scratched, the burned, the scraped or gouged; she was raised in and among the scratched, the burned, the scraped and gouged. Moreover: she apprenticed with Aunt Marveen, thrifter extraordinaire, developing a trained, discerning eye by means of exhaustive field experience. In any Goodwill, Salvation Army or consignment shop, at any flea market, Miss Jane is infinitely capable of spotting—and snatching—the unwisely dumped. With Prof P in tow, these salvage skills are compromised. Essential to Prof P's creed: shabby *must appear shabby* to demonstrate intellectual superiority / contempt for the conspicuously consumed. In the nearest-to-Bishop-Street thrift emporium, Prof P serially rejects un-chipped china, a sturdy pine table and comfy chairs in favor of: two (stained) mattresses (one to serve as sofa) and a plastic tub's worth of variously abused kitchenware. At the cash register, handing over a twenty, he reminds Miss Jane she owes half of that expenditure. Because Miss Jane does not agree, disagree or otherwise activate

41

her facial muscles following the pronouncement, Prof P decides to make a "lesson" of his equal treatment convictions. Hence: upon the in-house floor-lying sofa-mattress, midnight comes and goes as the chivying continues. Did Miss Jane *truly* want him to *pay the entire amount himself*? Assume *full responsibility* for her bed and board? Behave as if she were a *helpless dependent, incapable of taking care of herself*? Did she learn *nothing* in *HIS* women's history class? At which point glassy-eyed, sleep-deprived Miss Jane *surely* blinks, having learned many a thing in that women's history seminar, much of which she is still trying to parse and reconcile with her current predicament. Propped on a secondhand mattress, forced to stay conscious, our Miss Jane is harassed and decidedly fatigued. But she's not brain dead.

So give us the goddamn blink.

3.

Among the family, Miss Jane's eldest brother—and only he—is aware of her Bishop Street living arrangements, a secret contained between bro and sis for in what Brave New World could farmer dad and housewife mum comprehend this chunk of Unfortunate Events? (Or any Prof P chunk, come to think.) Contractor by trade, Miss Jane's bro can construct anywhere, including closer to the sis who may (ahem) need the assistance of a brother *nearby*. (Protective bro? Heaven's preview gift.) *We* certainly are relieved the relative who can lift his weight in two by fours relocates ten miles from the sis who emphatically needs an ally—blood kin or otherwise. Bro on the scene, next order of business: wheels for the sis who can no longer take the sidewalk to class. Because Seth B and Miss Jane are parted, not estranged, it's a trio that goes used-car shopping, Saturday morn. *Wait a miner's minute!* you're thinking. *If the gal can't afford half of twenty, how can she afford a car however used?* We refer you back to heaven-sent bro, who straightaway fronts the cash. The find itself: Seth B's doing. One owner / low mileage / new tires / 400 bucks, maintenance records included. Others might haggle; Seth B has done the research. The only missing piece is whether our Miss Jane feels at home slipping into the driver's seat of a Ford Falcon station wagon. Absolutely she does. She's been steering Fords since yay-high, her kin equally divided between stiff-dirt farmers and Ford plant linemen.

In life ever after Miss Jane will recall her first glimpse of that buggy: freshly washed white exterior, recently vacuumed blue interior, three-on-the-tree straight shift, her soon-to-be ride shaded by oak leaves, breath of breeze stirring the air. In it, a napping girl could stretch out full-length, no need to pull in her knees. In trilby and tweeds, the retired physics dean bids his mechanical mate an emotional adieu. Seth B bows his head, in car church. Miss Jane's bro shakes the sorrowing seller's hand. Swooningly happy Miss Jane succumbs on the spot to travel trance, travel visions. In a car one might go anywhere there are roads to travel—*anywhere*, including beyond a Bishop Street driveway. Regrettably, final term public university, South Atlantic region, the anywhere Miss Jane travels is bipartite, restricted to campus jaunts and work forays. For our Miss Jane, as often reminded by Prof P and never by her bro, lives currently in arrears.

4.

Clearly a job is needed—and not just any job. Miss Jane must find a part-time gig that won't interfere with classes, involves a task she can perform (or competently fudge) and nets her a *weekly* paycheck because Prof P insists her contribution to household expenses materialize in the cookie jar no less seldom than every seven days to sustain the fiction that they, college prof and college senior, are equally-funded equal partners. To her fifth interview, Miss Jane wears a maxi skirt, hair tied with leather string, asks no questions, tells no lies, nods at the end of each sentence her interviewer manages to utter between sighs. A listless depressive on the best of days, the branch manager of Tractor Trailer Training finds interacting with clients / staff debilitating, conducting interviews agonizing. The naked neediness! The expectation that a job offer will lessen woe! The pressure to select one candidate over the next! "Are you *comfortable* cold-calling strangers?" Miss Jane nods. "You'll be totally alone here, four to eight." Miss Jane nods. "The handwriting on the application cards is abominable. Impossible to decipher." Miss Jane nods. "Sometimes the salesmen just pretend to meet appointments. Sometimes they get to a house, turn around and drive home." Miss Jane nods. "Your job will be horribly dull. Are you sure you can stand it? I couldn't. Stand it." Miss Jane nods. As it happens, Miss Jane finds the job neither horribly nor remotely dull and stands it just swell. She enjoys being alone in a dark office, one desk lamp her beacon. Enjoys reviving the Christmas cactus neglected by the last four to eight-er. Enjoys deciphering smudgy directions on the order of: "Cow pasture to the left, barn on the right, path's a little overgrown but anyone looking ought to be able to find it." Icing on the cake? The year-older-than-Miss Jane part-time salesman / aspiring musician snags her a free ticket to see...*Joni!!* And the carriage belonging solely to Miss Jane? Runs like a top, drives like a dream.

5.

Are we pleased that Miss Jane experiences un-critiqued pleasure four hours a day, five days of week? Natch. Do we wish she'd compare / contrast / draw her own conclusions regarding the where and when of that bracketed contentment? *Fervently*. Must we shove aside (dashed) hopes and return to the home-front debacle? We must. For there our Miss Jane struggles on. In addition to her assigned reading for the semester, Prof P's supplemental list contains the titles of volumes with which (in Prof P's opinion) any college grad worth her self-respecting salt should be familiar. *Beowulf*. Buber. Carlyle. Casanova. Congreve. Whether-God-exists Diderot. An alphabet of books, all of them heavy lifting. We're not against expanding horizons; we're certainly not against *reading*. But come on! Given the pupil, why not lead with cabin-in-the-woods Thoreau? And, by the by, Prof P, where are the *women* authors?!? Miss Jane dutifully opens each and every book Prof P insists she must, but: distracted by a sliver of light, a squiggle of green, the dancing dots of peripheral vision, her mind drifts; it drifts. Would it have drifted less, assigned the poetess who penned *Nature murmured to herself / To keep herself in Cheer*? We'll chance an affirmative, Emily D no foe of the mental roam. The other poetess Emily, that take-no-prisoners Haworth dame? We're of two minds. Much as we adore ferocious EB, her self-eviscerations (e.g., *I am more terrifically and idiotically STUPID than ever I was in the whole course of my incarnate existence*) are nothing our Miss Jane should pour over in these perilous times. Any way you cut it, Cracker-tough ain't Brontë-tough. What brand of tough is?

In addition to extracurricular reading, Prof P *strongly suggests* Miss Jane audit his Labor History class, Monday-Wednesday-Friday noon. By noon Miss Jane is famished, classroom-pinched, preferring any outdoor roost in weather inclement or fair. Nonetheless, Monday-Wednesday-Friday noontime, look and ye shall find our girl cooped up in Prof P's overheated Labor History class where Prof P, irony-free, dissects the exploitative evils of power politics to another batch of long-haired girlies via flirt and tease.

Oh.

Wait.

Is this the point? Prof P's malefic objective? Introduce Miss Jane to the *competition*?

Crikey! How low can a juvenile middle-aged man sink?

Leagues lower.

Leagues.

6.

Time to meet the Family First.

Returned from visiting the grandparents (Park Ave. / Pound Ridge), Prof P's progeny are overdue an overnight with Dad. Miss Jane overhears Prof P's side of the telephone negotiations as well as an occasional dulcet reply. Already, from afar, Miss Jane is awash with admiration—not of the motherhood aspect, of the preternatural calm. She cannot imagine a mother of two—ages nine and eight—so even-tempered; she cannot imagine an ex-wife so amiable. In short: Miss Jane cannot imagine Lynette. And why should she be able? Lynette defies imagination. Classically beauteous, cheekbones like swords; philosopher by inclination / academic degree; serves squab for dinner; plays the flute. Sublime, astonishing, extraordinary Lynette is also, FYI, a saint. How many Miss Janes, before, after and during divorce proceedings has she endured? Countless, countless. Not unreasonably, she expects to meet her ex-husband's latest playmate before releasing her children into their joint care. En route, Miss Jane chews her hair. As she and Prof P approach the spectacular / cul-de-sac / glass and beam two-story—built by Lynette's current husband to showcase his Klees— Miss Jane loses feeling in her toes. How *dare* she share air with Original Wife / mother of B & B? When Dad and Miss Jane arrive, the noses of B & B are stuck in books and remain so while the short-term invaders pass through their rec room space. Perpetually invading B & B's space: two stepbrothers who live with their dad because their mom lives in a nut house. (Yes: Saint Lynette is also raising a loony woman's children.) Introduced to the saint in a scentless kitchen where orchids flourish, Miss Jane rocks on insensible toes, flushed with distress. The cause(s): jangled nerves and supreme self-consciousness—sure. But at its most basic, Miss Jane's upset springs from bewildered confusion. Why would Prof P or any man / woman throw over the divine / divinely accomplished Lynette for *any* newbie? (Why indeed.) With cordial aplomb, Lynette escorts swaying Jane to the Danish Modern sofa, returns with a glass of filtered water. Prof P? Too busy smirking to be of use. "I'm so sorry," Miss Jane stutters—conceivably for the faux pas of her near collapse, more likely in apology for existence. "It's quite all right," Lynette assures. "We all get a little light-headed now and again." Light-headed? Discombobulated? Exquisitely poised Lynette? Impossible! Unearned kindness undoes Miss Jane, always has. On Prof P's ex-wife's elegant sofa, Miss Jane's ears pound, her heart constricts. Hereafter, there is no snipe, no snub, nothing lovely Lynette could inflict upon Miss Jane (and nothing will there be) capable of altering Miss Jane's exalted opinion of The Original.

You of a more suspicious cast? Wondering if saintly Lynette secretly wonders whether her ex has knocked up the woozy creature on her sofa, more stepkin gestating? No. Lynette's focus remains on children already delivered; her thoughts, these: of all the girl toys paraded in her face and behind her back, Miss Jane appears to be an improvement. Whatever B & B will encounter in the company of their father's latest companion, it will not be a young woman's knee-jerk sense of contemptuous invulnerability and therein an implicit mother mock. In plain Jane, lovely Lynette perceives quite the contrary configuration: an acutely vulnerable soul. And who better than The Original to assess the disadvantage of vulnerability in a relationship with Prof P?

"Are we going or what?"

B & B are in no hurry to interact / lift eyes in the direction of Papa's newest "friend," but they are ready to *get on with it.* "You have a lovely home," Miss Jane mews in departure, by which she means: *I will not presume, encroach, impede; I will be naught in your children's lives,* receiving in response a gracious smile and thank-you. Adversaries? Not these two. Both said and unsaid: thoroughly understood.

7.

Time to meet the "dearest friend."

Along with Miss Jane, we revere lovely Lynette and resent any being, male or female, who causes her pain or trepidation, severe or fleeting, past and present. Of note: shed of Prof P (shared children notwithstanding), lovely Lynette is largely spared pain / trepidation spurs. Whereas philosopher saints may take the high road, we're prepared to drag down and dirty for any person / persons who deceived or colluded in The Original's deception.

Introducing—ta dah!—Joan C, Prof P's "dearest." Thumbnail sketch: Wellesley alum; director, social justice nonprofit; mother of morose teen; ex-wife of poet who, fed up with her critiques of him / his poems, fled the scene. In consequence: divorcée Joan is sole owner of a smashing Dutch Colonial, bought and painstakingly restored in the early stages of harmonic matrimony and in whose white, light-drenched kitchen she now brews a pot of bitter, bitter tea. For yes, (hot) tea is to be served alongside the living room's grand piano and maidenhair fern. Run-up to the meet and greet: Prof P's explication of the "evolving" interface between him and the dearest. Although he sought "simple friendship," libidinous Joan C pined for an exchange of genital fluids. As a "friend," he obliged, once, twice, "perhaps a dozen times," but his prick did not fancy Joan C's stretched snatch. Among the many details Miss Jane endeavors not to hear / register: the smell emanating from Joan C, point of orgasm, which Prof P, ever the gent, describes as "old-woman foul." (Reminder: Joan C is Prof P's contemporary.) Although Joan C's daughter is also at home, soirée hour, brooding in her bedroom, she is not invited to share tea with the adults and (barely older than she) Jane. To be more precise: Miss Jane entered grammar school the year Joan C's daughter ejected, womb to world, father's poem-in-progress speckled with placenta, mother unrecognizable in the absence of her exceedingly chic (frame-wise) and exceedingly dense (lens-wise) specs. When her trademark glasses *are* in place, Joan C's eyes are exceedingly magnified, rendering her peerings über-peerings. Peered at, Miss Jane neglects her tea, fearful of its journey tray to lips. What if it spilled on Joan C's Oriental rug? What if she oafishly disturbed the exactingly coordinated ambiance of Joan C's lair? Joan C's voice, a narcotic mix of purr and malice, is as hypnotizing as her gargantuan eyes and Miss Jane—conversation's topic but excluded contributor—*does* feel drowsy. Drowsy and thirsty. "I would have suggested Proust." "Her high school French teacher showed baseball films. You can't imagine how pathetically *behind* she is." "How dreadful. Who could envy such a creature?" (The she-wolf speaking, for one.)

Displeased that we're tarring / feathering poet-abandoned, odoriferous Joan C? Concerned about our politics? Be concerned about hers. In addition to talking over the head of Miss Jane (currently), she bedded The Original's husband (back when). Still not convinced? How about this? Without qualm or regret Joan C will anytime / anywhere throw any woman under the bus for prick / prick "friendship." Given the gleam in Joan C's magnified eyes, Miss Jane should already count as casualty. So why isn't our gal flattened, crushed and bleeding out on Joan C's Oriental? Because in the peculiar, singular case of Miss Jane, Joan C perceives the superior advantage of a different course of action. (Did you hear us disparage the woman's intellect? You did not.) Tea cooling, light fading, daughter retching, the hostess of the hour reaches out to stroke the plenteous mane of Miss Jane, conspiratorial smile coalescing. If she can't be balding Prof P's main squeeze, dear, dearer, dearest Joan C of the dyed, dry locks will strengthen their bond by contributing to Prof P's dearest cause: dicking with the hick / chick who is.

Ta dum.

8.

Time to meet (kindlier) Prof P affiliates, Yalies A &
E, English Restoration and popular culture scholars,
respectively.

In A & E's Marimekko-blooming home, Miss Jane is
handed her first glass of sherry which tastes, to her
uncultivated palate, much like cough syrup, the associ-
ation working in her favor. Who chugs cough syrup?
While she sips, A & E talk (though not exclusively)
university politics. Neither as awe-inspiring as lovely Lynette nor as treacherous as Joan C (due to arrive momentarily), A & E nonetheless expect dinner
guests to "contribute to the conversation." Paving
the way, Prof P embellishes tales of outhouse void-
ing and yard-fowl neck snaps—experiences of which
he knows nothing nor has Miss Jane shared. Thanks
to Prof P's intro, Miss Jane attracts the undivided attention of popular culturist E, eager to learn more
about "farming community rituals." Red-faced from
cause other than sherry, Miss Jane would rather not
sing for her supper, but such is required of swamp
natives at academic dinner parties. (Silver lining: Joan
C is running *very* late.) Offering help in the kitchen—
first course avocado soup—Miss Jane is for the first /
only time alone with scholar A, who, spooning milky
green, suggests Miss Jane write about her "exotic up-
bringing." Exotic? Pen-worthy at this advanced Year
of Our Lord? Do stereotypes *really* need reinvigorat-
ing? Hasn't *Tobacco Road* covered the territory just fine
for all time? For postprandial entertainment: charades!
And not just any sort of charades. Self-assigned charades, the better to reveal cleverness / lack thereof.
Despite stacked odds, Miss Jane's spirits (temporar-
ily) soar, buoyed by her sure-to-please choice. Sorry,
Janey. You're hanging with the wrong crowd. Taking
the floor, again and again Miss Jane mimes Patty /
Tanya swinging a semi-automatic to incomprehen-

sion. Us? Even with Joan C's huge eyes upon her, we think Miss Jane does a bang-up job conveying capture costumed as liberté. And why not? *Capture Costumed as Liberté* could be / should be a Miss Jane tee.

9.

Time to meet the inamorata who came before.

Work shift completed, Miss Jane returns to her nominal home, 8:23 Wednesday evening, tripping on the back step because Prof P "forgot" to leave on the outside light. To which we blurt, as we are so often apt to blurt regarding Prof P initiatives: *crap-ola-ola.* Miss Jane has entered a scene duly and truly staged. Inside: candlelight illuminates the mattress-couch upon which huddle / cuddle the entwined shadows of Prof P and ex-student N, back in town for…"oh, the weekend, maybe," Ms. N vehemently anti-schedule, schedules in concept / execution "so yesterday" and thus: *how absurd!* to conclude she collided with Prof P leaving campus in twilight's last gleaming via appointment versus chance. (To N, we extend the courtesy / insult that she too may be serving as pawn on this soundstage.) Rendered intruder in her own rental, Miss Jane cannot think how to (politely) mitigate that intrusion: stumble forward? Wait where she stands for the groping to cease? Turn and skedaddle? Ever / always in favor of *Skedaddle, Miss Jane!,* we are less surprised than she by Prof P's imperious: "Jane! Don't be rude! Come meet N." Background data: the one and only time Miss Jane got her legs switched with a quince branch, her mama detected rudeness on the part of Miss Jane toward Aunt Selma (who deserved it). Rudeness and punishment brain-linked, Miss Jane makes haste to un-do the offense by flopping cordially alongside N and Prof P, bright smile affixed. In the indulgent manner of a parent interrupted by a kid on date night, N also smiles. Since last she sat in Prof P's classroom or sprawled beneath him on his desktop, N has traveled to Mykonos, to Copenhagen, to Vienna, to Dublin, to, to, to… explorations continuing. "Always the adventurer," Prof

P coos, stroking *something* on the woman. In flickering candlelight we can't see exactly what—but we get it. As does Cracker hick / chick Jane, who is...let's call it *concerned*...that a threesome romp on one mattress or another is pending and N so tan and lithe, muscles hiked hard and Miss Jane so...none of those. If it were just Miss Jane and N getting it on, Prof P locked out, denied peephole privileges: yeah-a! But. We don't "arrange"; we report. Remaining where it remains: Prof P's half-mast dick.

10.

So, yeah. Sex.

We haven't forgotten about it either. If Prof P's boner isn't waving hard and high with two lovelies competing for his "reward," what's his stand-up percentage with single, drifty Jane?

You do the math.

11.

Exceedingly well-lit, Miss Jane's homecoming the following job-done evening. Light show's purpose? Spotlight the ogre. (Oh, all *right!* Prof P.) "Hiya!" hollers our gal. (Narrative imperative: girls waylaid by ogres lead with chirpy, time-buying, how-de-dos.) "I just spoke with N." (Total lie. N is on a night flight to Honduras, unavailable to chat / console / contrive.) "That's nice," replies our Miss Jane, peering into the refrigerator, trying to conjure there a slab of meat, preferably fried. "Nice?" Prof P's smirk plays to no advantage; Miss Jane's head remains in the refrigerator. "Would you care to know what she had to say about you?" Because Miss Jane continues her foraging, the ogre is forced to come to her (i.e., the creep creeps closer). "I believe the phrase she used was 'mediocre in all aspects.'" (Total lie #2. In N's universe, Miss Jane isn't important enough to rank.) "I actually felt quite humiliated on your behalf." (Ogre puts his hoof in it there. Even in a made-up conversation, a wise beast would avoid "humiliated" and its connotations. After all, whose flesh humiliated whom a very short while ago?) Miss Jane has yet to participate in / recoil from Miss Jane Bashing, Round X. The girl's *hungry*, for godsake. Likely faint from lack of carbs. "I thought we had some cheese..." Jerked backward, Miss Jane emits a feeble squawk. "No cheese! You know you can't eat cheese." (More on that idiocy anon.)

12.

Truly by chance Seth B and Miss Jane elect to browse Record Bar vinyl, same hour, same day, Miss Jane in a *world-that-can-be-sort-of-heartless* Karla Bonoff phase, Seth B re-smitten with Hendrix. Prevented (because he's Seth B) from asking after Miss Jane's physical / mental health, he instead inquires after her car, as in: "How's the car runnin'?" Simple enough question— the question Seth B actually voices—though Miss Jane can't seem to alight on any definitive answer, elaborate or concise, driftier than usual. Also thinner—to Seth B's practiced eye. Driftier, thinner—both observations accurate. Prelim to serving as photographic subject in the buff, Miss Jane has been placed on a no cake / no bread / no cheese slimming regime by Prof P, the "Renaissance man" who has apparently forgotten his Renaissance art as well as his Arbus. From misery, starvation or the enervating mix, second floor, Record Bar, Miss Jane lists toward Seth B, who leads her first to Arby's (where she downs roast beef with gusto), then to his garage for a check on the station wagon's oil and water levels, fan belt wear and tear. Drifting her way to the garage stool—still there! still waiting!—she halts, reaches out, palm-brushes another waiting-for-her perch.

Climb on, Miss Jane!

Settle your fine-sized ass on that motorcycle's leather seat!

Seth B will drop all to take you for a fresh-air spin, you know he will!

What he'll not do?

Presume to rescue a distressed maid unless / until that

61

distressed maid requests his help.

And Miss Jane doesn't ask; she doesn't ask.

13.

After a strenuous day in the sun—wood, screws and wood and screw men for company—the bro comes to dine with Miss Jane and Prof P. For his sis, he brings a basket of fresh asparagus and snap peas; for his sister's paramour: nada. Pleased beyond pleased to have her favorite bro within hugging range, Miss Jane twice leaps from her chair to squeeze his neck, prompting Prof P to admonish: "Ja-me! Really!" So now Miss Jane's a Ja-me? Since when? Saturday. Until when? Impossible to predict. The Renaming Project remains in its early stages, Prof P's other-than-Jane tryouts ongoing. In the thankful-for-small-favors category: Goody Jane? Not on the list.

In the aftermath of a) Prof P's reprimand and b) Ja-me nonsense, Miss Jane's bro squints, something—or someone—sticking in his craw. Though likely fantasizing the nailing of Prof P limb by limb to his chair, Miss Jane's "raised right" bro won't verbally assault / insult a man at his table. In order to wash down the god-awful whole-grain / brown rice drier-than-dry casserole concocted by Prof P for the occasion, he does, however, require extra fluids: a glass of water in addition to his glass of iced tea. A request easily fulfilled? Did you forget Prof P's "thrift" at the thrift store? Miss Jane reddens, rises, leaves her plate of lettuce to empty the contents of her own glass into the sink, scrubs, dries, refills that container with ice and water and returns it to her bro, who squintily drinks, thinking: a) no Cracker, struggling or flush, lives short of drinking glasses and b) the man nattering on about geodesic domes is a *professor*, paid whether or not corn prices take a dive or combines explode.

In the driveway, saying goodnight, Miss Jane avoids

looking her bro in the eye while squeeze-mauling his fingers. "Thank you *so much* for coming." "Since when does a sis thank a bro for visiting?" Since when has a bro-tease failed to trigger a grin? This night. This night. "You know you can always…," he offers before Miss Jane kisses his knuckles, shakes her head. Next morning, back step, a carton marked pointedly, prominently, **JANE**. Inside: a matched set of drinking glasses whose eight un-chipped rims Miss Jane also smooches before rinsing. Where to store the new, the pristine, the uncontaminated, from censorious Prof P? Miss Jane finds a place.

Did you catch that?

Miss Jane finds a place.

14.

Unwilling to celebrate that wee rebellion with a bouncy high-five? Losing patience? Baffled that hiding glassware represents the zenith of Miss Jane's independent actions to date? Wondering why our girl doesn't just *snap out of it* since she's not brainless, not missing a foot, perfectly capable of striding toward a car that varooms, other venues of shelter available to her (bro's trailer, parents' farmhouse, Cinda G's couch, Seth B's bed) and what's more: a jailer-gone opportunity this day, Prof P proctoring finals, her own (take-home) exams done, diploma all but in the mail...

Seriously? You're *seriously* asking why this bachelorette of arts won't climb out of her current life hole and be on her way? You *seriously* imagine there exists a simple, straightforward, uncomplicated, non-labyrinthine answer to that (utterly naïve) question? We'd have to interview half the college-degreed women on the planet to arrive at anything close to consensus, and we haven't the time, we simply haven't the time, Bishop Street roundup pending.

Re: Miss Jane's "relationship" with Prof P's urchins. On those occasions when each is forced into the company of the other, Miss Jane keeps her (unspoken) vow to lovely Lynette, initiating nothing, offering no advice, casting no vote in any colloquy involving bedtime, snacks or dubious behavior(s). For their part, B & B continue to communicate in a code devised to circumvent whichever transient occupies their father's bed. (Nothing personal, Miss Jane.)

Re: the curious case of Joan C. Driftiness seems to have bested Prof P's lubricious accomplice. Serially summoned to the Dutch Colonial for hair strokes, hot tea, "heart-to-hearts" and big-eyed hypnotics, Miss Jane proves neither forthcoming about her relationship with Prof P nor riveted by Joan C's fan-freak collection of letters and postcards from "influential people."

Re: the photo sessions wherein Miss Jane's long locks "artistically" drape some (though not all) of her privates. On and on they go. Does the model feel admired? "Empowered"? Are her nipples excited or just cold? (No, no and: just cold.) As subject-object of Prof P's lens, Miss Jane…disassociates—there but not there. Increasingly, during Prof P humpings and post-coital postmortems, Miss Jane also checks out from the reality assigned. Is she a prude? Is she frigid? Is she a cock teaser—or just a bitch? Not a prude, not frigid, not a cock teaser / bitch and not turned on, Miss Jane floats atop ocean waves, seagulls cawing, enjoying the scent of salt (not semen). Infuriated by inattention to his person by anyone / anytime, the *gall* of a Cracker hick / chick's indifference in bed sends Prof P into a pounding frenzy. His attack raises welts on Miss Jane's buttock.

Do we need another reason to revile Prof P?

We do not.

And yet the asshole supplies it.

15.

The world's tide bearing (us) along, we now surrender to the temptation to exaggerate / overstate / willfully inflate any inkling of defiance enacted by our Miss Jane. Case in point: where is she? Avoiding Bishop Street, we contend.

At the local mall, Miss Jane roams in and out of stores, up and down aisles. Competitive spending? Copycat shopping? Hardly. To acquire A & E's Marimekko-ed walls, lovely Lynette's orchid forest, Joan C's tea reserves or N's cache of halter tops would require infinitely more disposable income than Miss Jane's twenty-hour-a-week job provides. Two mall services that do fall within her price point: cut-rate haircut, unhygienic ear piercing. "How much off?" quizzes the clipper, hoping for the same instructions Mia Farrow murmured in her Frank Sinatra phase. Whacking done, Miss Jane's shoulders are visible but not her ears. Pain factor, ear piercing? More than Miss Jane was led to expect by the piercer-in-training, but no more than she can bear. Was Miss Jane's money well spent? We'll list the outcomes, you decide:

- Less hair to wash;
- Less hair to dry;
- Less interest from Prof P in photographing a bobbed-hair girl with infected ears;
- Less interest in bedding same.

When not mall roaming, Miss Jane takes to taking in matinees, suddenly fond of sitting solo in daytime darkness. Working her way through a box of Jordan Almonds, she thinks what **she** thinks—no discussion, no *corrections*—about script, lighting, theme, score, performances, the odd insect laboriously picking its way across the silver screen. A sampling of Miss Jane's un-shared thoughts: Jane Fonda does not a convincing Lillian Hellman make; the "intimate" cutting scene, *Cries and Whispers*, is not conducive to Jordan Almond crunching. Post-matinee this day, Miss Jane heads to her bro's place, outskirts of town, there to porch-sit with bro and hounds till hoot owls hoot. Before leaving the house: she pens no note. At her bro's trailer: she makes no courtesy call. Once returned to Bishop Street, she spends the rest of the night in her car, sleeping soundly. At the Ford's bumper, morning light, a ranting Prof P condemns "driveway camping" as the childish / selfish act of childish / selfish Miss Jane. Amid flailing arms and flying spittle, Miss Jane does not blink. Neither does she apologize. She (bonus points!) yawns.

16.

Returning the last of her library books, Miss Jane strolls a campus quieter than quiet. During the hiatus between semesters, the quad is defined / redefined by trees, breeze, the occasional squirrel, and this day by our Miss Jane, meandering at the pace of a grazing goat, pausing here and there to stare down at clover patches, up through oak-leaf weavings. Strolling her way: Prof K in his usual suit and tie. Sartorial choices are one way to distinguish Prof K in groovy tie-dye times. Another: he's Leon Trotsky's double. (Can such resemblance in a Russian history scholar truly be a fluke?) "Jane! Hello! Good morning!" Does the warmth of Prof K's greeting set your teeth on edge? Relax. Despite Leon resemblances, Prof K is neither a womanizer nor (more's the pity) interested in radicalizing our Miss Jane. He *remembers* Miss Jane because he recently graded her take-home exam on the Russian Revolutions of 1905 and 1917 and his database mind flags *any* student who excels, whether or not her origins be peasant.

Prof K receives our stamp of approval because: 1) he doesn't hit on / sleep with students; 2) at the departmental cocktail party Prof P insisted Miss Jane attend, Prof K deflected associative hostility toward Miss Jane by sharing his crudités; and 3) already generous with his praise on the returned paper, semester over, grades recorded, Prof K reiterates the praise. Has Miss Jane considered graduate school? Miss Jane has not. Prof K offers to pen a laudatory recommendation should ever she feel so inclined. Red as a raspberry, tongue-tied with pleasure, Miss Jane stutters. "That's...you're... very kind." "Nonsense!" (A bit of imperious Leon in that sharp rebuttal.) "You're an exceptional student. You deserve..."

Since Prof K is collegially prevented from finishing

that thought, we'll do the honors. Miss Jane deserves better than grody Prof P.

17.

As extra proof that ours is not a witch-hunting cartel nor our mission the indictment of faculty en masse at Miss Jane's alma mater, we sign off this section with the reappearance of another pro-Jane prof: the magnificent Carolyn Z, closing up her office for the summer, booked on a flight to Tuscany. Flopped on the steps of the Humanities building directly in Carolyn Z's exodus path: derailed Miss Jane, attempting to imagine the unimaginable (i.e., grad school).

"He put the Belt around my life / I heard the Buckle snap," The Magnificent bellows, cutting (as per usual) directly to the chase. As her erstwhile pupil swivels, Carolyn Z is also treated to the sight of butchered strands and crusty lobes, mutilations that inflame The Magnificent here and now as well as in perpetuity. *Why must women experiment FIRST on themselves?* (We're with you, sister woman!) In response to Carolyn Z's sharp query—"Summer plans?"—Miss Jane hems and haws. Carolyn Z *loathes* hem and haw, recognizing that sidestep for what it is: frightened female diffidence. "This is your *time*, Jane. Make every moment *count*. Go where you've never gone." (Far from Prof P!) "Do what you've never done."(Far from Prof P!) "Explore the continents. Explore yourself."

Inside scoop: competing for Carolyn Z's attention on the grit and grime steps: the ghost of Carolyn Z's former self, the Pacific Northwest girl she was and might have stayed: timid, reticent, mealy-mouthed, parochial. (Carolyn Z??? Timid??? Mealy-mouthed??? Present-day magnificence notwithstanding, do bear in mind: Carolyn Z is a woman of certain age born in certain-time America.) Mesmerized as always by The Magnificent's articulations, Miss Jane *is* listening. Raptly. Eyes ablaze, chest heaving, Carolyn Z leaves badly sheared / infected Jane to deliberate one last bit of matriarchal advice, and it's a doozy. "Remember, Jane: beauty is **not** an accomplishment."

Miss Jane! Where's your notebook? Find it! Open it! Write down Carolyn Z's wisdom for the ages!

Beauty is not an accomplishment.

Beauty is not an accomplishment.

Beauty is not an accomplishment.

Then ponder what is.

Interregnum

1.

Why "interregnum"?

What else therapy?

Because Miss Jane does not instantly get the hell out of Dodge, Prof P suggests (read: *demands*) she "seek help." Help to flee Dodge? Not a chance. Head-shrinker help. Therapeutic delve-and-dredge. Goal: twenty-two years of secrets / grievance / metamorphic-to-piddling decisions and misdeeds dissected, "re-contextualized," suspended in the amniotic fluid of mental health counsel. Twenty-two years of nature's relentless forward stymied in its tracks, time and life freeze-dried and shat out for inspection in a room without wind or clouds or trees or worms or biting chiggers. Twenty-two (somehow negotiated) years leading up to this pry-and-probe intervention by a licensed stranger because, in Prof P's (un)professional estimation, Miss Jane has "issues." Miss Jane is "emotionally blocked." Miss Jane is "lying to herself" and (therefore) to him.

Root cause of this swing in emphasis from Miss Jane's intellectual failings to Miss Jane's psychological dysfunction? We're not *positive*, but we *suspect* (yet again) Prof P boredom. Having convinced our Miss Jane— despite *other* professorial assessments—that she's an ignoramus nonpareil without the chops to ever "catch up," Prof P now sets about undermining his live-in's gut, by which we mean Miss Jane's belief that judgments communicated via her gut are inviolably true. (Note: Crackers, as a tribe, live and die by reactive guts.) Laid out thus, do you begin to comprehend the *depths* of Prof P's perfidious villainy in launching this latest traitorous assault? Miss Jane's gut is not only her lodestar, it's her inheritance.

75

But Prof P's not a therapist, you're thinking. *He'll not be in that windless, miteless room orchestrating the give and take. He'll not be IN CHARGE.*

Did we forget to disclose?

Turn the page.

2.

The therapist "chosen" for Miss Jane by Prof P is Prof P's childhood pal. Known each other since attending P. S. number whatever back in the burg of Manhattan. Other intertwinings: Therapist T, in her adopted hometown, barbeques with A & E, "treats" Joan C on Tuesdays and Thursdays and serves as godmother to B & B. A bridesmaid at Prof P's wedding, Therapist T remained friendly toward the bride only so long as she remained Mrs. Prof P, lovely Lynette dropped from Therapist T's address book / social clique the very day of divorce. (Does lovely Lynette give a shit about Therapist T's rebuff? We think not. We think not.)

Since Miss Jane's therapy is a Prof P scheme, adding lucre to the coffers of his crony, might he be picking up the tab? Are you *dreaming*? (Sheepishly) asked by his sis for the funds, Miss Jane's bro (squintily) shells out, likely assuming he's paying for an objective observer to officially declare what the subjective majority have long since concluded: Miss Jane and Prof P together? *Bad Idea.* Bad in theory, bad in fact, bad in the broad strokes, bad in the minutiae, big-picture/ small-picture / minute by minute / frame by frame, fundamentally, un-fixably BAD.

If Miss Jane's bro, *trying* to be less reflexively Cracker, is depleting his (severely limited supply of) Cracker optimism on the hope that closed-door sessions with Therapist T will extricate his sis from the Bishop Street bog, we feel terribly, terribly sorry for Miss Jane's bro—though not half as sorry as we feel for Miss Jane, due to convene with two-faced Therapist T.

3.

On Therapist T's sleek blond desk: scentless eucalyptus. On the wall: artisanal weavings. On the floor: artisanal cushions. On every flat surface: wads of Kleenex, the inventory in toto sufficient to sop up a small lake. Therapist T's yellow pads? Thick as Miss Jane's discomfort.

But enough with the atmospherics.

Let's get to the meat of it, shall we?

Although Therapist T's decision to focus on Miss Jane's dreams *seems,* on the face of it, therapeutically defensible, is it? The interpretation of dreams such a *sliding* art. The interpretation of dreams so interpreter-driven. The interpretation of dreams the best excuse out there for talking symbols versus incontrovertible facts. Choicest fact: Prof P is a louse of the first order and Miss Jane needs to start thinking **ABOUT** and **FOR herself, PRONTO.**

In the therapeutic domain, Miss Jane is also given assignments. Cough up a dream for a this-is-what-it-means consolation prize.

Will Therapist T's interpretations align with the interpretations of Miss Jane's talking heads (i.e., us)?

Rotter's chance in Zion.

4.

Dream #4— *"Classroom"*

As recalled:
Green, demonic-looking teacher. Student on first row fails to answer question. Demonic teacher wails on him. Panicked, Miss Jane and the other students flee. BUT. When the bell rings, Miss Jane returns, finds an open suitcase. Hers. Contents (white bobby socks, birth control pills) scattered.

As interpreted by Therapist T:
Miss Jane feels "inadequately schooled."

Our interpretation:
Demon correctly identified.

5.

Dream #7—"*Naked*"

As recalled:
In bed with Prof P. A noise wakes (still dreaming) Jane. Very short female and very tall male hover above the bed. Prof P wakes to chat. Miss Jane remains nervous. The front door is locked; the back door is locked. How did they get in? Prof P slides over, invites "their guests" to join them between the sheets. Miss Jane tries to cover herself with a hole-y blanket. No success.

As interpreted by Therapist T:
Miss Jane is "unwilling to share"; Miss Jane is ashamed of her "imperfect body."

Our interpretation:
Miss Jane doesn't care for Prof P's coterie.

6.

Dream #9—*"Trapped"*

As recalled:
Untold thousands squashed in a cave, Miss Jane among them. From a slit above, water pours in. Someone—not Miss Jane— begins to claw and climb toward the light, slips, falls, screams.

As interpreted by Therapist T:
Miss Jane is "willfully withdrawn."

Our interpretation:
Miss Jane is drowning.

7.

Dream #10—"*Dung*"

As recalled:
Miss Jane really, really, really has to GO. But where to find a functioning toilet? Not behind this door, not behind that. Not down this hallway, not out back. Commodes jammed, overflowing, spilling piss and crap. Rivers of excrement and Miss Jane caught in the flow.

As interpreted by Therapist T:
Miss Jane is feeling (wait for it)…"guilty."

Our interpretation:
Miss Jane is knee-deep in shite.

8.

Dream #13— *"(Almost) Dead"*

As recalled:
The fam gathers in preparation for a funeral. Miss Jane's coffin is already on the dock, tides churning beneath. The preacher is there. The choir is there. The dogs are there. People are crying. Mounting pressure on Miss Jane to "hurry up and die."

As interpreted by Therapist T:
Miss Jane is "disappointed in herself, as are others."

Our interpretation:
She's not dead yet.

Also: we're done with dreams.

9.

Miss Jane's Doodles

Prior to therapy session #1:

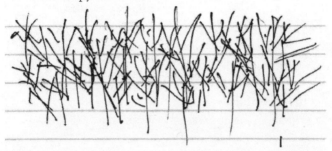

Prior to therapy session #4:

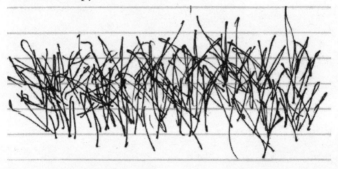

Prior to therapy session #13:

Not a lot of "interpreting" required, is there?

The girl's hemmed in, surrounded, in a dark, dark place.
Lost, our Miss Jane.

Lost.

Island O

1.

It's mid-summer in the Piedmont (i.e., unmercifully hot). Air still as stone. Lethargy a survival tactic. Miss Jane's ever-reactive cheeks stay rash-red morning to sultry night dripping sweat, no balm for prickly heat. For her Coastal Plain of origin, moist body / stifled breath Jane longs. Home is calling her home. (Agreed, it's strange: a Southern damsel sent packing by rising temps. That said, we'll get behind any excuse that flings Miss Jane wide of Prof P's orbit.) When she announces—yes! ANNOUNCES!—she's off to visit her folks, Prof P sulks. Her given-notice employer sobs, his allergy meds screwing with his anxiety meds. Summer months, emotionally, he's a wrung-out towel. "But you were the ideal employee! How will I ever replace you?" (He won't. Finding a *second* ideal employee amenable to minimum wage doesn't happen outside of fiction.) In addition to sulking, Prof P hints darkly at retribution. Without a job, how will Miss Jane pay her half of Bishop Street rent? *If* she doesn't pay, he won't "hold her place"; he'll "be forced" to find another "roommate." Not that we wish that disaster on any woman, but: *by all means*, Prof P! Follow through on the blackmail! Consider our lost Jane your lost cause! Harangued, Miss Jane's rashy cheeks burn brighter, but her resolve to head east does not flag. It does not flag.

Has mad heat created Zombie Jane, her zombie-brain ignoring blunt / insidious detainer threats, her zombie-heart squelching every tender wisp of feeling for her blubbering ex-boss, against whom (normally) she bears no grudge? To reach the cooler Coastal Plain, Miss Jane appears steeled to drive through walls, fences, orchards, Fourth of July parades. With forty dollars and change—sufficient funds to cover gas, a mid-drive fast-food burger—she'll *take to the highway*. In the case

89

of medical emergency / vehicular mishap, she'll rely on the kindness of strangers.

Whoop!

She's in the car, hands on a blistering steering wheel; she's started the engine; she's backing out, head turned from the spectacle of Prof P's tantrum. She's got the windows rolled down, radio turned up. Driveway and 'hood behind her, she and the station wagon's tires are spinning off Bishop Street altogether.

Are our ears playing tricks?

They are not.

Miss Jane is *indeed* belting out a song, really lettin' 'er rip.

The last time Miss Jane burst into song?

Pre the onset of Unfortunate Events.

Pre the onset of Criticism, the Sport.

Pre the acquaintance of prick Prof P.

A marvel is what it is: Miss Jane accelerating, pounding the steering wheel, swaying in the driver's seat, singing her lungs out on this muggy mess of a day.

Mad heat be praised.

2.

Songfest still going strong, Miss Jane arrives at the farm with three-quarters of her funds intact. (She skipped the burger: a girl can't chew and sing.) Because she arrives unannounced, only the dogs are immediately aware of her scent and self. Critters batting at her thighs, she makes her way to the house. Mom's in the steamy kitchen canning tomatoes, stove heat amplifying day heat, the lot smelling to high vegetative heaven. "Jane, hon!" Miss Jane folds herself into Mom's folds for a sweat-sticky hug. "Want me to slice up one of these tomatoes for a sandwich?" Miss Jane surely does! Nothing beats a homegrown tomato; nothing. Add Wonder Bread, mayonnaise, sweet tea sweet enough to induce toothache, and you have the makings of Miss Jane's current feast. While Miss Jane feeds her face, Mom sloshes another batch of Mason jars into stinging, boiling water. Task-of-the-moment complete, she sits, pats her daughter's arm, smiles, waits. If her daughter has something to share, she'll share it. If not, not. "Is it okay if I stay awhile?" Of course it's okay! Better than! Because, smile-pats aside, Miss Jane's mama is troubled by the look of her girl child. Beneath the standard red flush, Miss Jane appears... wan. Never a jittery sort, Miss Jane's jittery now. Darting up to wash her plate. Darting out to carouse with the dogs. Deciding she ought to *right now* hook hose to outdoor pump, wash and wax the station wagon, sun still high in the sky. "Whatever you think, hon," Miss Jane's once-again-stove-bound mom concedes, because that's who Miss Jane's mama is: "whatever you think" born and bred.

Twilight coming on, Miss Jane's daddy returns, the boat he's hauling filled with speckled perch. It's a contest, who'll get to Miss Jane's daddykins first, frenzied cats or hyper daughter. Tomorrow dad and daughter will settle in to watch baseball on TV, the slo-mo rhythms of the game helping Miss Jane ratchet down. (Absconding *does* require effort. But wouldn't it be lovely if, in the absence of Prof P, our Miss Jane didn't continue to suffer the *consequences* of Prof P?) Scaling fish or between home runs or sharing a porch swing—*some* where, some when—Miss Jane's daddy takes stock of the young'un beside him and breaks Cracker precedent.

You're shocked?

We're shocked!

Miss Jane is shocked!

Cats, dogs, chickens, cows, field mice and barn rats are shocked. We can only assume the *potency* of Miss Jane's misery, the pronounced *tremor* of her unhappiness, *compels* her male parent to ask the presumptuous, meddling question no self-respecting Cracker, given the choice, would ever pose: "You doin' all right, Daughter?"

3.

Although Miss Jane's pater may be up to the task of flouting Cracker custom, his daughter is not. Her daddy is her daddy. She shields him; he shields her. "I'm fine, Daddy," Miss Jane insists, a drenched-in-devotion falsehood incapable of fooling man or beast. To the unconvinced / lie-detecting faction we're inclined to add: Coastal Plain pine cones, gardenia blossoms, magnolia seeds, blueberry clusters and crabgrass. And if *flora*'s not convinced, what *can be*? Disbelieved by a cross-pollinated cast, Miss Jane's transparently bogus "I'm fine" has nevertheless been uttered. Can't change it, can't take it back.

Onward!

While breakfasting on fig preserves, Miss Jane scans the local paper, circulation 600. She's already checked the yard sale ads in advance of her outing with Aunt Marveen, but she's still chewing. By reason of prolonged chewing / scanning, she notices an offer of employment requiring neither welding nor reflexology expertise. To wit: chambermaid post, Motel Pelican, Island O. How hard can it be to strip beds, scour tubs and refill the mini-soaps? If the renters are slob fishermen on vacay, back-breakingly hard—but never-that-mind. The *important* point here, the *exciting* part, is that our Miss Jane is *sincerely* considering driving down two counties and hopping a ferry, prompted by fond and fonder memories of the fam's long-haul journeys to Island O to sun bake and wave ride when she was but a sprite of a thing. We've counted to sixty twice and neither the scorching Piedmont nor the devil squatting there has yet to divert Miss Jane's mind from Island O musings—a blip that, we're not ashamed to say, sends us into ecstatic euphoria. We're

93

leapin'; we're squealin'; we're dancin' the cha-cha-cha. Do it, Miss Jane! Doitdoitdoitdoit! Go be a chambermaid!

4.

In advance of her (new) job seek, Miss Jane throws us another curve: the girl buys herself a git-tar. On the scene, Miss Jane separates out a fiver from the thirty bucks in her pocket and goes home carrying. Marginally disappointed that her protégé skipped the haggling phase, Aunt Marveen can find no fault with Miss Jane's nose-out skills. (A fully-strung strummer for five bucks? Who could?) Back at the homestead, Mom packs a Styrofoam cooler with tea and snacks; Dad changes the station wagon's oil. (Foregone conclusion: one fine day Seth B and Dad *will* put heads together beneath a car's bonnet.) Most vocally opposed to Miss Jane's pending exit: the canine pack. Mom and Dad? Cheerfully resigned. Although responsible for Miss Jane's pipsqueak soul ditching the nebula to lodge in corporeal form, they serve as neither gatekeepers nor guards for their grown-up kids, their chore list already endless. As Crackers prone to underreport / undervalue / dismiss the quantity and quality of their contributions, they won't credit themselves; therefore, it behooves us to point out that (our and their) Miss Jane has grown plumper and less peaked since her homecoming. She's recovered (more than) forty winks, decimated plate after plate of fried foodstuffs, boldly purchased a musical instrument. In the brief time allotted them, Mom and Dad have done *wonders* restoring Miss Jane's vim and vigor. That's a fact. Now it's: *See ya later, alligator!* Guitar riding shotgun, Miss Jane toots the horn, heads off, curs her escort until dirt merges with macadam. Where's the map? No map required. Our girl knows the route, mucky peat to drifting sand, in actuality as well as memorious dream. Salty breeze wind-milling her hair, Miss Jane's got an elbow out the window, sweeping vistas of ecru dunes, cerulean sky, frothy whitecaps lining the sea her ancestors sailed upon three hundred-ish years prior, His Sacred Majesty Charles the Second "pleased to grant divers privileges" to "Honourable Persons" who'd "speedily plant" the soil of the "fair and spacious Province of Carolina"—*if* during the crossing those settlers-to-be survived dysentery, scurvy, Atlantic swells, cabin fever and the suffocating odeur of humanity confined.

Just sayin'.

Miss Jane's strain of Cracker?

Historically hardy.

5.

No need to waste suspense on this particular development: Miss Jane nabs the job, the beneficiary of a booming island economy and more tourist reservations than the Motel Pelican has seen in decades. However conscientious, two chambermaids can't service thirty rooms by three o'clock seven days a week. Miss Jane's new lodgings: mail carrier Mildred E's house. Other residents: Mildred E's scrappy tabby and assorted paying guests. To the attic room still available, cigarette dangling, white hair frizzing, the proprietress leads our Miss Jane. "Careful of your head." (A shortie herself, Mildred E doesn't need to duck.) "Not much, but what it is it is." (Mildred E's third line of work? Island philosopher.) Miss Jane *does* need to duck—head and shoulders—but doesn't seem to mind.

Us? We *love* the place! House full of femmes, Miss Jane's own private nook therein, window view of boats and sea oats, no Prof P. "Come to the kitchen once you're settled. We'll chat." As eager as any native to fleece non-natives, Mildred E, first glance, figures Miss Jane for a Cracker / Islander mix, mongrelized a few generations back. Mail deliveries finished for the day, Mildred E intends to talk genealogy while guzzling Pepsi. This she and Miss Jane do to the former's satisfaction. "You a knitter?" Mildred E inquires, mounds of red and yellow and pink yarn fluffing up her sitting room and kitchen. "No ma'am." "Interested in learning?" "Yes ma'am." Branching out, our Miss Jane. Mildred E's so pleased her face fissures into another thousand wrinkles, her cig goes neglected. "What say we start in tomorrow?" Is childless, widowed Mildred E lonely? She is. Does she meddle in the lives of her boarding house lodgers? She does. Does she stand attack-ready in the face of any threat to "her girls"?

Fuck yeah. Mildred E's a bulldog masquerading as an ancient. Away from the stifling Piedmont, away from Prof P, learning the git-tar, learning to knit and pearl, on salary, under Mildred E's protectorship: these the conditions of Miss Jane's precarious state of grace.

6.

Because Miss Jane is and always shall be a team player, she gets along just dandy with her chambermaid comrades, both of whom are worked to a frazzle though less so once Miss Jane starts scrubbing / Hoover-ing alongside them. Because Miss Jane—without quarrel or being asked—pitches in to help scour fishy-fisherman rooms not assigned to her, those comrades tolerate—more than they otherwise might—moments when, like seaweed in the tides, our Miss Jane drifts, gazing at the blue Atlantic instead of tucking sheets. There's a non-tourist bar off the beaten path (of course there is!) where Miss Jane and crew hoist a few, shift's end. There's the pleasure of returning barefoot in moonlight to Mildred E's. There's the pleasure of being snug in her attic bed, pleasurably weary, pleasurably buzzed, listening to waves roll in, roll out, roll in, roll out, sans the excruciating late-night histrionics of excruciating Prof P.

On her days off, Miss Jane patronizes Better Read Than Dead, a two-room bookstore with porch, deck chairs and owner who likes to see people reading books, whether or not those books are subsequently purchased. Free to make her own selections of reading material, Miss Jane, we notice, sticks to poetry by her kind. Exhibit A: *Went into a shoe store to buy a pair of shoes / There was a shoe salesman humming the blues.* Exhibit B: *This Englishwoman is so refined / She has no bosom and no behind.* Admit it! You're amazed that the Island O bookstore stocks Josephine Miles and Stevie Smith. As are we. As are we. Lord love the indies. Afterward, Miss Jane lugs her guitar to a patch of shade near the marina and plunks away. Like a million other Judy / Joan / Joni aficionados, Miss Jane aspires to what she can't achieve, her technique atrocious and unlikely to improve. Nonetheless, *she*'s enjoying herself until her plunking draws the interest of boys on the lookout for long-haired girls with requisite guitars. Do you imagine her audience to be long-haired as well? Recalibrate. The holiday boys who encircle Miss Jane are shaved and barbered frat-ers in white shorts and boater shoes. Surrounded, Miss Jane immediately shuts down her practice session. "No! Don't stop! Keep playing!" "I'm just learning." "You sound great!" (Memo to Lying Guys: clean / cute / privileged doesn't automatically equal convincing.) "Excuse me," says our Miss Jane, stepping over ankles, another girl interrupted from what she wants to be doing by interruptive guys.

Cinda G visits. That's a treat. In and around Miss Jane's Motel Pelican hours, the duo "lay out," get sun-roasted, gorge on flounder, fry themselves up a batch of hush puppies. Taught to knit by her granny, Cinda G joins the Mildred E / Miss Jane knitting circle and finishes a pink-red-yellow scarf in rapid time. Whenever the house phone rings, Mildred E—and only Mildred E—answers. "Boy. Seth Something. For you." The speed at which Miss Jane comes running? Mildred E notices. The tabby notices. Christ, even the window shades notice. But does our Miss Jane?

7.

Does Miss Jane invite Seth B to visit or does he come of his own accord? Undisclosed mystery. Mildred E, watching the August 1 reunion through cig clouds from her doorway, assumes what, we hazard to say, anyone with similar viewing privileges would assume: *it must be love* (or the Perry Como equivalent). However the convergence transpires, we're awfully, awfully glad that once again Seth B's within striking distance of our Miss Jane. The flesh knows what the mind denies. From ferry to town on Highway 12 Seth B and Miss Jane zoom, sand dunes on either side of their migration. When Miss Jane and Seth B stroll the docks, frat boys make the snap (and not erroneous) judgment: *so THAT's her type*. In his summer stage of being, Seth B appears shaggier, less leather-ed, his baby blues paler amidst island blues but no less a steady-on fellow at peace with himself and the curious ways of a curious world.

What?

"Steady on" offends you?

Insufficient sturm und drang for your taste?

To each her own, but what we observe, Seth B back on the scene, is this: Miss Jane at her ease. Un-cowed. Un-apologetic. Unashamed. While Miss Jane puts in time at the Motel Pelican, Seth B crabs and collects lumber wash-up for their nightly bonfire. Regardless of prevailing winds, tidal charts, barometric pressure readings, he beach-sleeps. Night Two of Seth B's visit, Miss Jane joins him in his bedroll, the pair waking to empty shores and a yellow dawn. No, no. We're not being delicate or evasive. Seth B and Miss Jane go carnal on the night (and morning) beach. And, gad, wouldn't we love to

101

leave them there in romantic fade-out. Complication 1: possessing no frat boy trust fund, Seth B can't stay forever on Island O. Complication 2: summertime won't stay put either.

Seasons changing!

Tourists dwindling!

While we freak on her behalf, Miss Jane appears…copacetic, agreeably settled, looking forward to autumn's gale-force winds, electrical outages, moored ferries, Island O cut off from the mainland for weeks on end. Between tourists' departure and tourists' return, Miss Jane pleasingly imagines: yarn parties with Mildred E; Better Read Than Dead her second home; a frat boy-free marina; the Atlantic reclaimed by foul-weather fishermen; the whole of Island O populated by happy isolates. Would Miss Jane actually enjoy the wintering? Impossible to test. Already in place, the Motel Pelican's off-season staff: one chambermaid to accommodate vacationing stragglers, one handyman to board up windows and sandbag perimeters, duplications unnecessary. Sorry, Miss Jane: final payday Friday. Miss Jane receives the news as Miss Jane receives any news: with fatalistic compliance. At Mildred E's she collects her guitar. On the docks, unobserved and undisturbed, she strums and mulls, strums and mulls, sky overcast, air chilling. Quite obviously, the girl needs another job. (Now.) Very soon she'll need to give up the guitar. (Although, in that judgment, we're divided. What harm strumming, however artless?) This *instant* Miss Jane needs a sweater. (And needed one twenty minutes ago as well.) What she doesn't need now or ever is Prof P showing up on Island O, wrecking the independent vibe. But that's what happens. That's what the sleazebag does.

Stalker ahoy.

8.

In Mildred E's driveway, Prof P lies in wait, the proprietress having refused him house entry. (*Love* that woman. What set off Mildred E's radar? His age? His arrogance? His smarmy attempts at charm?) On the home stretch, Miss Jane and guitar lose propulsion, halted by the formation ahead. Is she really seeing the man she sees? Oh, Miss Jane! If only your predator *were* a phantom—or subject to spontaneous combustion, a bevy of naked women dancing around his ashy nevermore. Instead: the too-real Prof P jogs toward Miss Jane's stunned stillness, a contrived smile on his conniving face.

New setting, new Prof P strategy: fake groveling (to start). *So, so* "contrite." *So, so* "ashamed" of his "previous" asshole-y ways. *So, so* "bereft" without Miss Jane, his heart's desire.

Pardon us while we barf.

And you! Quit hoping a Cracker hick / chick will prove *the* catalyst for *genuine* Prof P reform. Prof Pees don't change; they self-replicate.

Body-trapped, Miss Jane's mind whirls in sync with the agitated gulls above. *Why* is he here? Working hypothesis: the summer has not gone swimmingly for Mr. All-About-Me. Example: on his recent trip with B & B to Pound Ridge, his father and stepmother a) demean his paltry publication record, b) smirk at his "always inappropriate" attire, c) upbraid him for the umpteenth time for divorcing lovely Lynette, and d) in his presence instruct B & B to abjure a career in the lowly humanities. Browbeaters taught browbeating at daddy's knee still qualify as browbeaters. Active example: "I've missed you *every, every* second of *every, every* day! Don't you *care, care, care?* When are you coming *back, back, back* to *me, me, me?!?"*

Goddamn the Motel Pelican's policy of skeletal winter staff! A cash-strapped woman is a vulnerable woman. Glaringly excluded in Prof P's dragooning: any pledge to alter future behavior (see previous paragraph #4), oath swearing of any sort not the ace up Prof P's denim sleeve. Prof P's diabolically sly bargaining chips are: a rental in the country, daffodils in the spring, muscadines in the fall, fields of alfalfa and Miss Jane's bro a scant mile up the road. To turn aside the inducements of daffodils, muscadines, fields and bro-as-neighbor, Miss Jane would have to be other than the Miss Jane standing on Island O's shifting sands.

Despite the vociferous objection of screeching gulls, shit-bombing the shit beside her.

Despite the appeal of coast and yarn and unfettered horizons.

Despite a week of waking to sand and waves and Seth B's loyal, loving member.

Despite the sight of Mildred E on her front porch, adamantly shaking her grizzled head.

Despite.

Despite.

Despite.

Miss Jane will reside on Buckhorn Road.

Buckhorn Road

1.

Geez, Louise and Geez, Louise and *Geez, Louise!* It is and was our wish to avoid yet another domicile, town or country, selected or inhabited by the blackguard Prof P. Yet here we find ourselves, the same as Miss Jane. To the apologists keen to remind us Prof P's "not doing so great either," not feeling his omnipotent oats *quite* to the extent he felt that grain in yesteryear, we can only presume we previously failed to make our position / prejudices screamingly clear and hereby repeat with flugelhorns: Prof P's feelings? **Not our concern.** Should, for half a second, the reigning bastard of this tale second-guess his bastard self, his despicable treatment of our Miss Jane: **too little too late.** We're not in the business of kindness or mercy. We're self-anointed avengers.

However.

Since our concern covers Miss Jane's health and well-being today as well as tomorrow, we're scoping the place for anything that might contribute to Miss Jane's *current* comfort while keeping an eye firmly on the prize (i.e., bye-bye, Prof P). It *is* a larger house. Separate kitchen. Separate living room. A bedroom for B & B. The (usual) room allotted for Prof P's exclusive use. A (non-marital) bedroom for the full-time occupants. During an earlier, truncated residency, the mortgage holders painted the outside of the house fire engine red, perhaps as l'aide à l'emplacement among interlocking greens. Once they return "to the land," their offspring no longer of age to be de-potentialized by county school inferiorities, (possibly) they'll adjust that palette, retirement funds permitting. We'd also recommend an exorcism to rid the place of Prof P's ectoplasmic ick—but that's just us. Helping the new tenants move in: Miss Jane's bro and pickup truck. And because Prof P does not / will not check the operating status of water pipes, sink drains, fuse boxes and septic systems, Miss Jane's bro carries out those inspections, his sis absently rewashing every dish Prof P ever touched. Absently because, apart from her hands, the rest of her is mesmerized by views of barn and meadow, oak and maple, a wire clothesline identical to the wire clothesline on which her mama still strings up *her* household's washing to dry. The luxury of a Buckhorn Road clothesline means our Miss Jane will again sleep on air-dried sheets. In the annals of Cracker mythology, air-dried sheets have been known to: a) reduce the effects of migraines and heat stroke, b) keep lice and ticks at bay, c) improve sinus congestion. They have yet to be thanked for breaking up a home, but where there's precedent to be set, precedent will be set, yes? The bro's side business—furniture restoration— means there's a surplus of venerable rockers hanging from pegs in his shop. One claw-handled beauty with double-scooped seat he gifts to his sis. While her bro grins, Miss Jane undertakes the task of finding precisely which spot this instantly prized possession will occupy. To that end, she drags, angles, sits and rocks while the idle Prof P observes. The idler's first mock, the bro lets slide. Not so the second. "We got this covered." Cracker code for: *Get the fuck out of here, dickwad, my sis is having fun.* In (half) compliance, Prof P strolls toward a porch once screened, now glassed, to declare the space "useless."

Au contraire.

Once Prof P wanders out, Miss Jane and the bro wander in, banks of windows revealing leaf and sprout and vine. Plenty of green inside too, compliments of a monster philodendron left behind by the owners, no townhouse corner spacious enough to embrace its sprawl. Sentiments to note: Miss Jane harbors no objection to CO2 / O2 exchange with a monster philo-dendron nor is she rankled by the owners' decision to glass-in the porch to enable all-season usability at the expense of summer's blow-through breezes. In fact, our Miss Jane has no quarrel with the room at all, at all. It's precisely the abode for her bro's fine rocker. Once bro and sis tag-team that beauty across the threshold: more good news. The bro thinks he'll be able to whip up a nifty side table since he's "already got the wood."

Quick tally: Miss Jane's chair, Miss Jane's table. A room *with* room—and scads of it. A bright space with no dark corners. A bright space *at the far end of the house*. With a *door*. That *closes*.

Such rooms hold promise.

Such rooms hatch confidence.

It would appear we underestimated Buckhorn Road's subversive opportunities.

(Our bad.)

2.

Perhaps because B & B are unimpressed by their near-empty bedroom upgrade, perhaps because Miss Jane's close-by kin has re-categorized in Prof P's noggin as dangerous in a *Deliverance* / who'll-hear-a-New-Yorker-scream? sort of way or **maybe** because Miss Jane decides on her own, without *discussion*, that the Buckhorn Road house will be a *furnished* house, she sets about making it so. Mind you, the result is décor neither new nor matchy-matchy. It is, visually and chiropractically, an improvement over floor mattresses. The wood-crate couch comes courtesy of a neighbor's giveaway. Farm table, steamer trunk, iron bedstead and oak dresser are junkshop raids, carried out by Miss Jane in the company of her bro. If the accumulation displeases Prof P (it does), he refrains from saying so in the presence of Miss Jane's champion. Are we pleased that Prof P's intimidated? We are. *Terrifically* pleased.

Downside: Miss Jane's household expenditures further deplete her bank account, an outcome / ongoing circumstance harped about (in the bro's absence) by Prof P in his usual niggling way. Nobody—Prof P, Miss Jane, Miss Jane's bro, sparrows swaying on electrical lines—disputes her need for income. But the chances of finding employment that pays stupendously and fascinates utterly with a bachelor's degree on the outskirts of a university town, semester kicking in? The topper-most Miss Jane can hope for are a few hours of reimbursed drudgery here and there. At the Registrar's Office, she collects course cards for incoming frosh. For the Psych Department, she views videos, noting incidents of "family conflict." Although our Miss Jane excels at collection, she sucks at conflict reportage. A Cracker *girl* child, she's been trained since diaper-wear to look above and beyond simmering disputes / resentments, conflict

110

avoidance the Cracker female's special province. (Let the lads duke it out!) The ordeal of black-marking clashes between mother and father, parent and child, child and child turns Miss Jane queasy. When queasy, Miss Jane resorts to drift. Adrift at her Psych Department job, Miss Jane feels dishonest, guilty, a slacker. In September, the South Atlantic region remains hot, hot, *hot*. Atmospheric warmth + embarrassed contrition = red wreck. And that's not the worst of it. The psych tech in charge (no conflict avoider, he) declares Miss Jane the "worst conflict marker in the history of the project" and fires her ass. Severance check in hand, flush-faced Jane looks above and beyond to...under-employment. Cinda G's solution: Kelly Girl. In the local Kelly Girl office, Miss Jane details her hire-me credentials on four separate questionnaires before submitting to a typing test. Typing verdict: slow but accurate. Despite those underwhelming results, the KG manager declares she'll "go out on a limb" and assign Miss Jane to the university's provost office. Snazzy office—for campus. Table lamps (as opposed to fluorescent strips), mahogany desks, wall-to-wall, echo-absorbent carpet. Hunkered in front of an IBM Selectric, 24-pound vellum rolled and ready, Miss Jane is drilled on office policy and procedure. No typos. *Absolutely* no Wite-Out. Every scrap of outgoing correspondence triple-checked to ensure flawless accuracy. Tap, tap, tapping, Miss Jane sets no speed records but does achieve a slow, steady rhythm. Miss Jane's trial completed, the assistant to the assistant to the provost proofs every line / word / comma, as do two of her compeers.

Success!

Miss Jane's a keeper!

Or was.

Until.

Under the guise of "support," Prof P "drops by" each and every day of Miss Jane's inaugural week. By interrupting Miss Jane, Prof P interrupts the assistant to the assistant to the provost. "How can we help you?" "You can't. I'm here to see Jane." The assistant to the assistant's incendiary glare is no deterrent to Prof P, who considers himself "faculty entitled." When directed toward Miss Jane, the assistant to the assistant's glare works only too well. Miss Jane's face is *molten*. "This will count as your morning break." What Prof P doesn't know that will hurt Miss Jane all the same: faculty status means squat to the provost office denizens; they deal with faculty by the hundreds. Point two: in *any* office unscheduled breaks do not endear. As a result of Prof P interference, friendliness sputters, long faces grow longer, hushed deliberations are conducted behind semi-closed doors. Yep, once again our Miss Jane's out on her ass, plus tarred and feathered by a bad eval. No Kelly Girl manager, out on a limb or otherwise, will risk sending her on a new assignment. Which means Prof P has sabotaged our Miss Jane's ability to stockpile cash.

Do we think this a random act of violence? We do not. Nor should Miss Jane.

3.

Construction guys (like Miss Jane's bro) know realtors. Realtors need bodies to sit in model homes. The bodies realtors prefer: "presentable" young women who can tolerate the tedium of sprawling all day in model homes without turning surly. Mel R's real estate office needs two such lovelies and two he gets: Miss Jane and Christine W. Right off the bat, we're charmed by Christine W, theologian's daughter, actress-in-training, her "baggage" at twenty-two encompassing ex-husband George, rusty VW Bug and full set of wedding china off which to eat her Food Stamps-subsidized frozen dinners. A profane and spirited blondie, Christine W likes to cackle—and pretty much everything on God's Demented Earth makes her cackle, including Daddy the Theologian. When her previous handsy employer calls her "well-preserved" (at twenty-two), she cackles. When her landlady pot-searches her apartment (who can afford weed?), she cackles. Caught shoplifting juju beads, she cackles—then sprints. When Prof P shows up at the model home, she Blanche DuBois-es him around the foyer before maneuvering him out the door—a feat that makes her *and* Miss Jane cackle.

Miss Jane becoming chums with a gallows-humored, law-breaking ambitious divorcée who treats Prof P with cheeky disrespect? Answered prayer. The glitch? Showing model homes? Not a forty-hour-per-week engagement. Which means our Miss Jane is far too often lodged in a non-model home with non-model partner Prof P.

4.

Not that Miss Jane's base camp this season is totally without merit. It *is* located in the country. Shear off Prof P and pleasures abound. Free figs and plenty of them; front, back and side yards still green and growing. Mowing grass is Cracker hick / chick nirvana. Like her daddy plowing up / down, up / down, Miss Jane plying a lawnmower up / down, up / down is *in the zone*. Nuthin' gonna bother a gal *in the zone*. Other green alliances: Miss Jane and the monster philodendron's symbiotic relationship works splendidly (unlike other relationships in the household). Next to philodendron spread, the bro-built table lodges books and iced tea and Miss Jane's homemade flower press. Rocking as clouds puff and birds chirp, Miss Jane achieves the sort of self-induced oblivion we all hope for ourselves…at *ninety*. Miss Jane's *twenty-two* going on *twenty-three*. Get out of that rocker, Jane! Heed nature's lessons! Grow! Stretch! Overreach! Break free of the (Prof P) hedge!

Visitors who visit (not night-blind Joan C or country-phobic A & E) include Prof P's Aunt Dottie from Queens. Aunt Dottie bunks in town with lovely Lynette, whom she adores and continues to regard as legitimate kin. (If we were Aunt Dottie, we'd feel the very same.) With no small amount of trepidation Aunt Dottie makes the journey to Buckhorn Road. Purse clutched firmly, she endures a Miss Jane-guided stroll around the property in heavy dew. She cannot precisely remember Miss Jane's name (and why should she?) nor does she care for hippie casseroles (for lunch or any other meal) nor does she wholly approve of her hippie-esque nephew. Never has. She would have skipped the Prof P visit but doesn't quite see how to manage the snub without jeopardizing her reputation as genial Aunt Dottie. After Aunt Dottie departs lovely Lynette's guest bedroom, lovely Lynette's younger sis (Kelly) and Kelly's husband (Barry) move in. Bored with quiet evenings of faultless civility, they decide to "mix it up" with a drive "out to the boonies" to hang with ex-in-law Prof P. Since Kelly comes within a hairsbreadth of being as lovely as the consummately lovely Lynette, her perplexing marriage to short, brash, pug-nosed Barry raised eyebrows at the wedding that have not since lowered. "What's with this country living shit?" demands Barry upon entry. "Got any Coke?" Soda, he means (on this occasion) for Barry is trying to kick his nicotine habit by ingesting five to seven caffeine-rich Coca-Colas per hour. Luckily for Barry, Miss Jane's soda stash *never* dips below a case and a half; come the revolution, she will have caffeine to barter. While lovely Kelly feigns interest in Prof P drivel, antsy, un-narcotized Barry roams the house, picking up this and that, Joni's divergent *Don Juan's Reckless Daughter* one of his snatch-ups. "Like it?" Barry interrogates. "I will. I just need to listen more." Color us (and Barry) impressed. "Some albums are like that." Sensing accord where he'd rather not, Prof P pipes up: "I can tell rot from classic first time through." "Bully for you," says Barry. The lovely Kelly's response? Lilting laughter. Laughter that twirls and twits and twitters. At what / whom? We have our suspicions—and our preference. Relish the company of laughing women, Miss Jane! They know much refused expression in a bully-boy world.

5.

Symbolism.

It will creep in, even in a plain-Jane life.

Prof P teaching a night class (or plugging a new student), Miss Jane weathers the first autumnal storm alone. Lights flicker, windows rattle, a tetchy wind lets loose its ire. Wishing she had one of her mama's kerosene lanterns, Miss Jane assembles a blackout kit: flashlight, batteries, candles, matches, bobby socks (in case her feet get cold), transistor radio, her guitar because she's never tried to strum in the dark and in the dark maybe her strumming will improve... (It won't.) At 9:03, darkness obliterates Edison's contribution to civilization, recasting light as the underdog. Is our Miss Jane ill at ease, alone in a house deprived of modern amenities, her sanctuary rumbled over by thunder, streaked by kinked lightning? Nah. A fear of lurking marauders isn't the reason she's repeatedly, apprehensively, checking windows and doors; she's looking for the cat—a stray without home or shelter this blustery night. Directly disobeying Prof P's edict (yay!), Miss Jane has been feeding the ribby thing on the back steps, little by little earning the trust of a creature who's long since lost faith in the consistent kindnesses of weather or two-legged beasts. And now the drenched cat shivers atop a utility pole, chased to that outpost by a pack of pass-through hunting dogs prior to the storm.

It's a sight, it is: Miss Jane in soaked flannel, rain-blinded, arms raised, beseeching a mass of wet mewing to come *down*, come *down*, the beseeched unconvinced salvation lies in that directive or direction. In the rain, Miss Jane finds a ladder. In the rain, Miss Jane climbs it, gown-tail tied around her waist. "It's okay, it's okay,"

Miss Jane assures a living, breathing, tortured example of otherwise. For an hour, nearly two, in wind and rain and primeval darkness, it's a match-up: feline wariness versus Cracker resolve. And then, and then: a clawed skitter. When Prof P returns from doing whatever / wherever / with whomever, he finds Miss Jane and cat snuggled on the couch. Based on previous edicts, one might expect Prof P, in usual huff / puff fashion, to order the cat's expulsion. Hampered by makeshift lighting, we can't *swear* to it, but what we *believe* we see is a single raised index finger. Cracker-speak for: *not a fucking word out of your fucking mouth.*

Who / what to thank for this throw-down? Two hours spent in Lear-like supplication? Rescue-restored courage? Confidence imparted by rib-side purring? Whatever the inspiration, the results *tickle us pink.*

Darling femmes of the universe, rejoice!

Storm season is upon us.

6.

As in bedtime tales: *Suddenly! A knock upon the door! Is it friend? Is it foe? Who might this mysterious stranger be?* Granted, B & B no longer require reading assistance—*Piss off, peeps; we can bloody well read ourselves!*—nor are they this hour in bed. When the evening's extra guest comes a-knocking, they're at their father's supper table, grousing about the unappetizing inedibles on their plates. As children of divorce, ever-alert to goings *and* comings, B & B give the door and the unknown behind it their full, snappish attention. The cat and Miss Jane? Kitchen-bound. If the door is to be opened, Prof P must do it. (Heh, heh.) Outside, the sky retains a streak or three of light, red and yellow leaves drifting branch to bramble. The two guys, astride either side of the Buckhorn Road threshold: still points on a swirl-y stage. "I'm a friend of Jane's," says—yahoo, yahee!—Seth B. Even above noisy dish clatter, Miss Jane hears, *knows* that voice, its timbre, its twang. Her dash toward it freaks out the cat and confirms what B & B suspect on the broader scale: Miss Jane's a runner. Just like their father's last live-in and the one before that and the one before that. "And your *name*?" Prof P needlessly quizzes, Miss Jane squalling "Seth! Seth!" as she barrels past the bluff-meister's barricade.

"Can we talk?"

Rock and hard spot, eh, Prof P? Everyone "free" and "equal" here. Miss Jane *entitled* to her friends / space / privacy.

Through the picture window, B & B, cat, and Prof P cannot fail to observe: close bodies, syncopated rhythms, the unmistakable harmony of *this* fellow and *this* gal in *this* landscape-surround.

Moving to the country / reuniting Miss Jane with her country familiar(s)?

Big mistake, Prof P.

Big mistake.

Heh, heh. Heh, heh.

7.

Another school year in swing, another wagonload of Miss Janes to plunder, you'd think Prof P would consider himself a man sittin' pretty, ridin' the wave, ball in his corner, ducks in a row. Instead Mr. Overindulged feels resentful, persecuted, his "giving nature" played upon by a Cracker hick / chick who with appalling deceit and knavish cunning (uh...hypocrisy, much?) separated him from his town, his friends, his precious, precious children, deliberately and with malice aforethought isolating him on this loathsome, hayfever-y acre of fleas and frogs and buzzards and by the accumulated aforesaid crimes and injustices *even at this moment* continues to gravely impede his "seminal, trailblazing" study of "gender history."

Nothing wrong with your eyes or brain or comprehension. You read what you read accurately. Prof P possesses a book contract to plumb "social and sexual interactions" between guys and gals Victorian era through "modern times."

Are you astounded?

Are you confounded?

Are you crying / laughing / sick to your stomachs / stompin' / spittin' mad that *this* man is being paid *good* money to expound on a subject about which his head is / has been (for decades) stuck up his ass? Take a number—then take heart. For *Her/Him/Them* (working title) is indeed not going well despite its author enjoying the expansive advantages of *two* rooms of his own: campus office and Buckhorn Road study. The problem: prose that "refuses to flow." Never before has Prof P's prose "refused to flow." Ergo: the cause /

cock-up is not Prof P. The author wants his editor, his publisher, his department chair, A & E, Joan C, lovely Lynette, Aunt Dottie, Miss Jane, her cat and **all of you out there** to understand that any semantic clogs are not *his* fault or failure; *he's* not to blame. He's the *victim* here. He's the one suffering. He's the one prevented from thinking / writing / sleeping. He's the one driven bonkers by cricket chatter and mosquito buzz. Word-blocked Prof P gnashing teeth, in the throes of book dementia, stewing in his own juice.

Nice.

8.

Coincidence or karma? Miss Jane joins a book group.

Heh, heh. Heh, heh.

It comes about thus. Scanning for job notices on her local library's bulletin board, Miss Jane spots a flyer announcing book group meetings twice monthly, midweek, mid-afternoon. Since Miss Jane's midweek mid-afternoons are *not* booked, she's free to join the klatch. Group leader Tulane M—recovering anorexic, published poet, Ann Arbor refugee—feels what she feels *intensely* and permits no half-formed / half-baked comment on any text to stand unchallenged. Her hair color, a flaming orange, does not come out of a box. When excited, she vibrates. Second-in-command Susan J traded in ballet shoes for motherhood several years back but remains the most upright of sitters / standers. In her whispery voice she offers whispery, scathing commentary regarding the success or failure of chapters, paragraphs, sentences and key phrases. Though not totally opposed to psychoanalytic interpretation, she despairs when that analysis falls short of eloquence. A former nail biter, a judicious distance separates Susan J's hand and mouth at all times. Mary Y, originally from Atlanta, is the only attendee who partakes of Miss Jane's "thanks for having me" mound of lemon squares. Mary Y rarely finishes the books under discussion, relying on her ability to "wing it" if cross-examined by taskmaster Tulane M. The very limit of Mary Y's patience for any comment, including her own, is a minute five. After that, her attention...wanders. "Welcome," says Tulane M, a cordiality extended to Miss Jane—not to her batch of lemon squares. "This fall," Tulane M declares, "we will read thematically." Miss Jane nods. "Mary, share your list with Jane."

- *Great Expectations*
- *Dracula*
- *Lolita*
- *The French Lieutenant's Woman*
- *The Scarlet Letter*
- *Tess of the d'Urbervilles*
- *Women in Love*
- *Madame Bovary*
- *Anna Karenina*
- *The Taming of the Shrew*

The Male Prerogative, 1590 to 1969?

Brides, Beware!—the Short Course?

Whatever the binding theme, Miss Jane is game to go the distance. Game, but anxious. While Tulane M holds forth, Miss Jane's gaze—along with Mary Y's—drifts, Miss Jane's toward library shelving. Will she be able to check out *every* title? No way can she afford more books. Not even the paperback versions. Not even used. No need to agonize, Miss Jane. Every public library in the country—no matter how podunk—stocks male canon "classics."

Finding these?

- *Fernhurst*
- *Nightwood*
- *Blood and Guts in High School*
- *Novel on Yellow Paper*
- *Serena Blandish*
- *The Stepdaughter*
- *Two Serious Ladies*
- *The Fat Woman's Joke*
- *By Grand Central Station I Sat Down and Wept*
- Any book by Laura Riding

—different story. But go ahead! Search! Prove us wrong! We'll be thrilled. Skeptical, but thrilled.

9.

On the porch, cat in her lap, book grouper Jane reads:

> A wonderful tenderness burned in him at the sight
> of her quivering, so sensitive fingers. At the same
> time he was full of rage and callousness.
> "This is a degrading exhibition," he said coolly.

> I saw that everything within my view which ought
> to be white…had lost its luster. I saw that the bride
> within the bridal dress had withered like the dress.

> Once or twice I had cast an appraiser's cold eye at
> Charlotte's coral lips and bronze hair and dangerously
> low neckline, and had vaguely tried to fit her into a
> plausible daydream. This I confess under torture.

> Nobody could dislike Aunt Tranter…. She had the
> profound optimism of successful old maids.

Not to forget:

> To leave her in farmland would be to let her slip
> back again out of accord with him. He wished
> to have her under his charge.

Miss Jane and cat (again) have the house to themselves,
no (exterior) storms predicted. If only Miss Jane and
the cat could *always* have the house to themselves. Or
themselves and specially invited guests Cinda G or
Christine W or (potentially amusing) Mary Y, or, or,
or. If only Miss Jane could *afford* a house of her own.
But what wild wish / plentiful funds pipe dream have
we slipped into? The most our Miss Jane can afford is
a tent—and not a swank one. A tent some other tenter
has parted with. A heavy tent. An awkward tent. A tent
that smells of piss and mildew…

Yowza.

Tent digressions.

We must really, *really* want to avoid Joan C, topic and presence, even as she sticks it (in the critical sense) to Prof P in her decorous living room, autumn's pale light expiring. Impetus of visit: Prof P has asked his dear friend to read and critique his "monumental" and monumentally stalled work-in-progress in order to revive industry, profundity and trip-along prose, objectives to which Joan C contributes via slicing and dicing the paragraphs that exist. Prior to schlepping his treatise to Joan C's Dutch Colonial, Prof P attempted to drop it off at lovely Lynette's glass and beam two-story, weaseling to have his ex-wife take up another chunk of unpaid labor on his behalf. Although lovely / brilliant Lynette is obliged to confer with Prof P on certain matters relating to their children, she is no longer obliged to read his manuscripts. *Hit the road, Jack!* To palm off the manuscript on a departmental colleague would be to: 1) give that colleague leverage, 2) risk mailroom gossip—powerful disincentives, no matter how elevated Prof P's desperation levels. Naturally the author would never consider asking the Cracker hick / chick he's shacking up with for feedback and for once he has our untrammeled support. *Great decision, dingus!* Miss Jane's brain is already male-d to the max with her book group list. She doesn't need to add your crossed-out, typo-ridden mumbo-jumbo to the mix.

Is Joan C monumentally enjoying herself—or is Joan C *monumentally* enjoying herself? Prof P hanging on her every word; Prof P, insecure and needy; Prof P in her house, in her thrall, for as long as she cares to keep him there, nitpicking apart his risible exegesis of the male / female "conundrum." Tutoring session done, will Joan C and Prof P retire to her shades of gray bedroom for a roll in the sack? (They will.) Will Prof P's "corrected" dick know what to do with itself once there? (It won't.) And thereby a lesson, femmies: always take payment from a knob in cash, never trade.

10.

Testosterone lit aside, Miss Jane's book group does allow our gal the opportunity to keep up her bulletin board browsing, the local library home to, count 'em, three such boards: one dedicated to jobs, one dedicated to services and one dedicated to animals. The posting that catches Miss Jane's eye appears on two of the three: jobs and animals.

In exchange for kennel duty (daily) and dog-sitting (occasionally), Margaret D is prepared to pay "the right person" handsomely and, should that right person be interested, teach her the basics of dog training (gratis). To call the listed number ASAP, Miss Jane risks the wrath of Tulane M with an "excuse me" bolt toward the outside pay phone. At Margaret D's house, Miss Jane is welcomed by a German shepherd, a schnauzer, a boxer, a sheltie and the diminutive Margaret D, a research scientist / dog lover who trains pooches that compete in (and win) obedience trials, regional and state. Instant rapport: as if Miss Jane and Margaret D were best mates in a previous dog kingdom. Extra employment bonus: Miss Jane gets to accompany Margaret D to dog-dedicated events, featuring canis lupus familiaris of every breed, shape, shag and color. What Cracker hick / chick in similar employ, granted similar perks, wouldn't consider herself one lucky bitch? Miss Jane comes to the job experientially well-schooled in curs, hounds, the number of water moccasin strikes to the head a pit bull mix can absorb before keeling over, the foamy effects of untreated distemper and the necessity of keeping shut the barn door when a pet's in heat. Under Margaret D's tutelage, she learns AKC-recognized breeds, AKC standards, telltale signs of hip dysplasia and the inadvisability of turning her back on Margaret D's hip-healthy German shepherd while cleaning his pen. She also learns the Blanche Saunders method of training pups to heel / sit / stay / come and lie down—in that order. Margaret D calls Miss Jane a "natural" whose dog handling skills and training instincts continue to improve by "leaps and bounds." Prof P complains that Miss Jane is "never home anymore." The cat smells dog on Miss Jane's jeans and…worries. As well the cat might. Margaret D also fosters shelter dogs. Inevitably one will come along to steal Miss Jane's stealable heart.

Don't pretend you didn't see this plot twist coming 45 pages back!

Those dogs???

In that dream???

When Miss Jane refuses to die???

11.

Miss Jane's imminent pooch is a ragtag mix of setter and labbie. A pup with puppy breath. A pup that whimpers. A pup without permanent home. From Buckhorn Road, Miss Jane brings sweaters and towels to plump up the laundry-room bed of Margaret D's temporary charge, installs a ticking clock to soothe the fretful. She cleans up pee, cleans up poo, hand feeds kibble, dark wet eyes watching her every motion. As would any Cracker, Miss Jane undertakes Mutt Intelligence Crosschecks. Does the beast dash forward or cower? Does the back of his skull rise to a bumpy crest? Delighted by her findings, Miss Jane's attachment grows. Soon she is hugging her new darling, nuzzling his nose. To leave him every evening is a tiny death. If Miss Jane's daddy were around, he'd draw the same conclusion as Margaret D: "He's your dog now." "You mean it?" Miss Jane stutters, afraid to believe in such beneficence. Afraid— and yet, and yet: does Miss Jane hesitate to scoop up the critter for his first car ride? Does Miss Jane, prior to that ride, consult with her co-tenant? Does whether or not Prof P will object / sneer / sulk / give her shit for bringing home an un-housebroken pup coalesce as concerns in the brain of giddy Miss Jane?

Nope.

Progress by way of pup.

12.

Ever so tired of describing the snits and tantrums of Prof P, we here provide a fill-in-the-blank.

*Miss Jane shows up with dog and Prof P*_____.

The cat, though. What about the cat?

Prolonged yowling followed by projectile vomiting. None of Miss Jane's peacekeeping efforts convinces the cat to trust the pup or his let's-be-buds overtures. (Do recall: the cat's been run up a utility pole by the very same species.) For advice, Miss Jane calls in the closest critter expert (her bro). "I'll find her a good home," says he. "She's not happy here." Yes. Those very words the bro speaks, supposedly talking cat while gazing meaningfully at his sis. Prof P—rid of one competitor by way of feline transfer—finds his status in Miss Jane's priority list unchanged, *all* of our gal's attention now devoted to the joyful, romping canine that considers her the bee's knees.

You consider that a distressing, pitiable development? Not us. Prof P's incorrigible. The dog can still be trained.

13.

Inside a week vigilant trainer Jane teaches Noon—for Noon he is christened—to trot to the door, lift a paw and drag it when seized with the urge to whiz or defecate. On his six-week b-day, despite the drizzle, Miss Jane and Noon repair to the yard with lead and choke collar, Miss Jane following Blanche Saunders's triangulated heeling strategies to the inch. *Good Dog! Good Puppy!* To please his mistress, if he knew how, Noon would turn back-flips. *Good Dog! Good Puppy!* To show off the mastered heel-sit combo, Miss Jane invites the bro to supper, which they consume on the porch, exiting the house via the back door for the demonstration. (Avoiding Prof P like the plague, we're saying.) Noon smells family on the bro, in no way spooked by the additional audience. Post-performance, Noon's rewards include: extravagant praise, Milkbone treats and forty-five minutes of fetch, Cracker humans as riveted as he.

Is that the shadow of evil / evil's shadow lurking at the window of Prof P's study, wondering what's happened to his fun and games?

What if it is?

What if it is?

With twice-daily training sessions—at Buckhorn Road, at Margaret D's—Noon speedily learns his stuff. If Miss Jane orders him sit / stay in front of his doggy dish until she's finished pouring, sit / stay he does. If Miss Jane warns him to sit / stay at the top of the dirt lane while she hoofs it to a mailbox, sit / stay he does. If Miss Jane insists he sit / stay until she's ready for him to leap in for a how-much-fun-is-this? grocery run, he obeys, delaying the gratifications of internal

131

combustion speed. Point of fact: if our Miss Jane set off for the moon or Vegas or the rodeo, devoted Noon would follow, toenails clacking, tail wagging. It's not the *dog* that's opposed to getting in the car or hopping a plane or strapping on a rocket pack to go, go, go / leave, leave, leave / be, be, be elsewhere. It's not the dog holding back Miss Jane.

It's not the dog.

14.

Winter arrives, ready or not. Season of shut-ins / shut-downs; trees, shrubs, bushes, briers holding on by playing dead. First a nip in the air. Then frosted grass. Then ice storms that snap branches, slick earth, send Prof P's Volvo skidding into the ditch. On three occasions, Miss Jane's bro arrives with truck and chains and frees the fellow who won't repay the kindness by driving his now drivable car off the face of the earth, releasing sis from the freakish spell she can't herself seem to dissolve.

Miss Jane has her dog.

She has her books.

She has her bro nearby.

She has her job with Margaret D.

She has the citadel of an unheated porch where, encased in two sweaters, three pairs of socks and fingerless gloves, she doodle-draws what *could* be the scene outside her window:

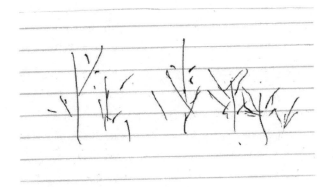

...or the bleak terrain of inner Jane.

15.

With the very *best* of intentions, the bro arranges a get-together with the folks: his place, dogs welcome. It's been awhile since two of the brood broke bread with Mom and Dad. Family time, the bro decides, will cheer up his sis. Swamp to trailer, it's a four-hour expedition (give or take), no particular hardship for early risers / late-to-bedders Mom and Dad. They'll be on the road by sunrise, aim to "be back around midnight." Dad keeps the speedometer "around fifty" so he can field-observe along the way; Mom darns socks because to "ride along doing nothing wouldn't make a lick of sense." They're spruced up, for Mom and Dad. New sports shirt and cap for Dad, Mom in her next-to-Sunday best. In the backseat: deviled eggs, Virginia ham, pecan pie—not because the kids "can't cook for themselves," because they love their mama's deviled eggs / Virginia ham / pecan pie and it would be "crazy" and "a shame" (i.e., a "crazy shame") to go "all the way up there" (sideways, actually) and "not bring something they like to eat." We agree, Mama! We agree! Hauled in the trunk: ancestral photos reclaimed from the attic, requested by Miss Jane. (Will that lineup of flinty-eyed Crackers give Prof P the creeps *and* the squirts? We can only hope.) The parents locate the trailer without mishap, following directions based on rocks, fence posts and "a big oak near the turn." It's winter but one of those winter days that heats up nicely, eleven to two. The bro shows off his customized barn; Miss Jane shows off Noon. "He's a smart one, Daddy," Miss Jane confides, beaming. "Can see that. You pick him or he pick you?" Cracker joke for a Cracker audience. Hilarity ensues. Then it's plate-loading time: Mom's goodies, bro's barbeque, Miss Jane's baked beans.

And will this loving family reunion remain undisturbed,

humans feasting, dogs cavorting?

It will not.

Clouds caucus. The wind picks up, distributing scent other than family. The dogs corral, prick up their ears, woof in warning: Gatecrasher! Trespasser! Nuisance on the grounds! Before mottling, Miss Jane blanches. The bro stands, advances. Mom and Dad look up from the table, prepared to be pleasant, prepared to scooch over, make room for another body, another plate, prepared to meet and greet a friend of their son's, an *old* friend of their daughter's, prepared for a *wide range* of variables, but in no way prepared for Prof P.

How could they be?

16.

Did Prof P's invite get lost in the mail / the bushes / the toilet? It did not. Bro's trailer, bro's guest list. A pointed exclusion that clearly didn't succeed since *here the fucker is*. Flexed and ready—one might say *eager*—to throw the uninvited out on his keister, the bro won't move a muscle without a signal from his sis in the form of, say, a half nod or lazy blink. Notwithstanding his personal shoving-match preference, whatever happens next the bro leaves to Miss Jane's discretion. Introduce the douchebag, pretend she's never laid eyes on him— either way, the bro's got her back. Count on it.

"Are these your *parents*, Jane?"

The bro shifts weight onto his toes; Miss Jane's voice squeaks. "Mom, Dad. This is…one of my professors. I think, Mom, the two of you spoke once? On the phone?" A stall—and whew: a lame one. But Miss Jane has *always* sucked at rhetorical / syntactical / farcical delay. Cut her some slack. She's doing the best she can in difficult circumstances, as are bewildered Mom and Dad. Alarmed by her daughter's trembly jaw, her husband's suddenly knotted brow, her son's not entirely unclenched fists, Mom manages: "Did we?"—her hazy memory adding insult to Prof P's injury. Why is his *eminence* not acknowledged?

Clarification: Miss Jane's not *afraid* of Prof P; she's *upset*. When upset, nine times out of ten, *something* on her quivers. On this particular occasion, she's *pro-actively* upset, knowing (as do we, as does anyone whose spent a millisecond in Prof P's company) that Prof P's not going to *take his cues* from the parties assembled. He's not going to *play along*. He's not going to shake Dad's hand or chow down on the last remaining piece of pie with compliments to the chef. Nyet. "Truth purveyor" Prof P's going to *tell it like it is*. He's going to *lay bare* the facts. He's going to *take a stand*. He's going to tear down the *fraudulent* walls of fraudulent *conspiracy*. He's going to unmask every lie of omission and commission. He's going to expose the cowards, hypocrites and hick / chick who dares *deny the existence* of truth-teller Prof P. He's going to *reveal all* to Mom and Dad, whether or not Mom and Dad prefer to know zilch about private lives, their children's private lives most especially. Prof P's going to bring every Cracker in the room *up to speed* about his role and shared-with-Jane residence because *right is ON THE SIDE of Prof P!*

As Miss Jane dreads, so it occurs.

"I *was* your daughter's professor; now I'm her lover."

Perhaps because the revelation fails to produce the desired results, Prof P begins to recite, with mounting fury, his "superior credentials," listing educational degrees, tenured status, the names and ages of his (seeded) progeny, pausing only to give baffled Mom and Dad the chance to applaud / thank him for bestowing his attentions on their backward, undeserving child. Such appreciation / gratitude is not forthcoming. Very likely, over the course of his entire pontificating life, Prof P has not encountered the equal of Mom and Dad's undeviating silence. For the cause of entertainment, Crackers will watch a fool make a fool of himself the livelong day. They're bred for the sport. Was any Cracker in bro's trailer this day entertained? Regrettably, no.

17.

Not an easy ride east for Mom and Dad. Dad forgoes field inspections; Mom neglects her darning. What they don't say, darkness descending, they think: their child Jane *seems* to be "caught up" with a fella who *seems* more concerned about himself than her. Next week, Dad will go fishing thrice instead of once; Mom will let the ironing pile up, lingering with the mutts on the lip of the porch, dangling her toes, staring at tree bark. But since Miss Jane hasn't asked for their help in escaping the muckety muck (and Miss Jane would swallow rat poison before making such a request), Mom and Dad feel duty bound to respect their daughter's right to deal with what she has to deal with in her own time, by her own devices.

It's the Cracker way.

But we're here to tell you as flies on the wall / ghosts in the galley / snoopers privy to the private Jane that this self-reliant / self-negating Cracker is in trouble. Deep and deepening trouble. In the immediate aftermath of the bro's barbeque, in receipt of her parents' mute and worried support, as witness to Prof P's Prof P-ness in the context of family reunions, our Miss Jane falters. She falters badly. Those ancestral tintypes we hoped would hairy-eyeball Prof P? From porch windowsills they're giving Miss Jane the business instead. Hefty women, scrawny men, no smile faint or full-blown to leaven weary and worn. Not a visage or bearing among them to suggest they expected more / other / better than worn and weary EVER. This is Miss Jane's heritage—this, her blueprint.

Exquisitely sensitive to his mistress's every mood and manner, Noon takes up residence at Miss Jane's unmoving side, head upon her knee, whimpering. As sorry as we are for Noon's reciprocal distress, we wholeheartedly endorse its expression. At least *one* creature on Buckhorn Road *should* give voice to despair because, as of now, Miss Jane is sticking with protocol.

18.

A profoundly painful dejection, cessation of
interest in the outside world, loss of capacity
to love, inhibition of all activity...a lowering
of self-regarding feelings...self-reproaches...
self-revilings...a delusional expectation of
punishment.

Though not keen to drag no-friend-to-the-femmes Sig-
mund into this, when a definition applies, it applies. In
our (non-Freudian) opinion, melancholia femina flour-
ishes in two strains: anxious and resigned. As a fatalistic Cracker hick / chick, the second is Miss Jane's fate
and undeniable condition. She passes on a reconnect
with Therapist T (no cash? no interest?), but to lack a
therapist is not (necessarily) to lack in nightmares.

For example:

Miss Jane, sunk in a pool, wearing pearls.

(Does Miss Jane own a strand of pearls? No.)

**Someone not quite strange / not quite fa-
miliar yanks Miss Jane by the neck / necklace.**

(Does sunken Jane resist? No.)

When Miss Jane surfaces, the yanker flees.

(Will the identity of the yanker be revealed?
No.)

**"He was trying to save me," Miss Jane ex-
plains to the woman reading** *Moby Dick* **in**

the lounge chair.

(Save or strangle? Unclear / unresolved.)

The woman shuts her book. "We're taking a poll. Should Ahab have died? It's time to render your first and final judgment."

(Does Miss Jane respond? No.)

Miss Jane re-sinks.

19.

And so it continues for our Miss Jane: soaked and soaking in melancholic waters by night; swan diving into melancholic lit by day. Her porch walls sprout paper streamers: quotable quotes from the poetically depressed. Keats's numbness, Coleridge's lonesome wild. Call us crazy, but we'd rather pinched lines from old guys offed by TB and infarction than Miss Jane's liftings from the how-to girls.

By which we mean *I rise with my red hair* Sylvia.

By which we mean *I have been her kind* Anne.

Although Miss Jane isn't (yet) a drinker, her next binge reading could pass as a primer in drunk lit, the genre. *Under the Volcano. Good Morning, Midnight. Tender is the Night.* Yates. Exley. Ernie. In spite of her melancholic stupor, farm child Jane tries doggedly to work out how impoverished characters flit off to bull fights with unlimited funds for unlimited booze.

Miss Jane phones Cinda G; Miss Jane phones Seth B. Into the receiver to each our Miss Jane whispers: "I am trying not to hurt anyone" (the exception to that charity herself). She phones Tulane M to apologize for her book group absence, to say she isn't sure when / if she'll be returning. Trying to explain why, her voice peters out entirely. "The hardest hours are five to eight," Tulane M commiserates. "Just focus on getting from five to eight."

20.

Miss Jane in her nightgown, three p.m.; Miss Jane's hair a hive. If you assume she's (also) chucking off weight by the handfuls, you'd be wrong. Cracker hick / chicks eat when depressed. Constantly. Sara Lee coconut cake straight outta the freezer. Peanut butter straight outta the jar. At the disgusting, repulsive, undisciplined, *ungrateful* sight of Miss Jane, Prof P rails and rants. So why doesn't he move on to less disgusting / repulsive / more grateful pastures? Can't think of an immediate answer? Take another crack. A fatty at odds with herself is that much easier to (choose one or five): disparage, demean, demoralize, brutalize, destroy. So do be sure to add to Prof P's list of dazzling charms his ready willingness to walk over / sucker punch / mind fuck a gal who's down, down, down. Photographs of Miss Jane from this era exist, but trust us: you don't want to see them. Driftiness without anchor. Blankness as membrane. Loyal Noon peering up at a mistress not fully aware of his presence or hers, faulty connection body to brain, belief in the operational here and now misplaced with yesterday's tissues. Sadness, the drip.

On Friday morn, Prof P announces he'll be dining with A & E, Joan C and Therapist T on Friday eve—with or without Miss Jane. (Is a woman barely able to speak the syllable that is her name in any condition to argue?) For *far too long*, Prof P's been "exiled" in the "unendurable" domain of possum and skunk. He *deserves* a night on the town.

Okay.

Bone toss.

Rural living's not for everyone. But who rented the

house and for what purpose? Are we suddenly supposed to feel sorry a scammer's unhappy, sorry that an ego-maniacal *manipulator* unwittingly screwed himself in the bargain?

On Friday at six, bathed, dressed and ready to commune with his townies: Prof P. Miss Jane? Not so much. She *has* pulled on a skirt and sweater but can't seem to find her boots. Infuriated by the delay, Prof P reverts to ranting, specific targets this hour: eye bags, chin pimples, the flab bloating Miss Jane's waist. She's hideous; she looks like a bag lady—she *smells* like a bag lady. She's a joke; she's pathetic; she's a complete and utter embarrassment *to him*. Is Miss Jane's slowed-down cerebrum processing? Is Prof P's tirade penetrating? Enough to prompt the removal of what cost enormous effort to assemble. Sweater, skirt, left sock, right, each item abandoned where it drops. In her underwear she returns to the bedroom, stretches out on chenille. When the front door slams, she's already away-away in her head. Our immediate reaction to the back of Prof P? Good riddance! One less misery in the house! But now…now we're feeling less sure about Miss Jane's status as sole human in the Buckhorn Road dwelling, losing confidence in the assumption that Miss Jane's aloneness this night is a situation to be encouraged or applauded. We're growing uneasy about the deep-dish silence and Miss Jane's interpretation of it. We're worrying Miss Jane might begin to confuse silence with nothingness—a nothingness personified. We're apprehensive that, in a noiseless, shadowed room, the body on the bed might begin to conflate its lie-in with *all my trials, Lord, soon be o-o-ver.* And so we're relieved that, unlike other houses occupied by Miss Jane, this one contains no .20-gauge shotgun, the Cracker weapon of choice for offing food / prey / oneself. We're relieved the ocean Miss Jane so adores crashes and roars four hours east. We're relieved Miss Jane doesn't daily stroll alongside an Ouse-ian river with fast-flowing, tempting tides. We're relieved Miss Jane stopped reading Virginia before reading:

Now, in my nightgown, to walk the marshes.

A curious seaside feeling in the air today.

So I am doing what seems the best thing to do.

We're relieved Miss Jane has collected no pocket stones.

And there our relief ends.

For even in the absence of guns and stones, water and Woolfian fiat, our Jane has come to harm.

21.

Apologies.

Miss Jane's distress has proved contagious. We suddenly feel as if we've been barking into a wilderness of *big deal* / *so what* / *get over it*. We suddenly feel as if someone of the non-female persuasion has sabotaged the communique, interrupted service with malicious intent. We suddenly feel outnumbered and underfunded.

Kindly permit us a recovery page.

22.

Let us say this. Let us say without reservation or qualification of any sort: we believe (Piedmont) country saves Miss Jane for as long as Miss Jane can be saved by forces beyond the perimeter of Miss Jane. Spring does its revivalist duties via jonquils and daffodils, tulip trees and meadowlarks. There are berries to pick and ticks to pluck off the ears and scruff of Noon. There are the unrestrained visual / textural / olfactoral idolatries of landscape to dazzle and distract a mind from its close and musty corridors. There are weeds to weed, grass to mow, sheets to air-dry—all beneath a shimmering sun. With her bro, Miss Jane plants a beans / cukes / squash veggie garden, devotes a fourth dug-dirt row to zinnias and marigolds. She cleans closets, cabinets; she reorganizes the shed. She washes the winter-streaked windows of her thawed-out porch. When the bro heads east for a spring planting assist, Miss Jane and Noon hitch a ride, her head / Noon's head sticking out the same window, road wind the intoxicant. Pit stop at Hardee's for sweet tea, leftover ice cubes Noon's treat. Miss Jane and the bro listen to the radio, startle field crows but mostly drive / ride ensconced in travel-induced contemplation / meditation. "You know how sometimes," Miss Jane ventures, pauses. (The bro's accustomed to pauses, short and long. What Cracker isn't?) "You know how sometimes it feels like…" (If the bro's in no hurry, why should his Cracker sis be?) "…when you're talking to people…" (The bro brakes gently for a stop-and-go squirrel.) "…and they're really only waiting for you to say something they can use to talk about themselves?" The bro nods. (Does he ever!) "It's just that…lately…I'm starting to think I don't like those people very much."

We're *so* pumped by the promising applications of this

at last uttered aversion, we could *pop!* Yes! *POP!* But the bro, the bro plays it cool. Doesn't say: "You expect to like everyone, sis?" Doesn't say: "Some people are dipshits and you live with the pick of that litter." Limits his response to: "Some people aren't worth liking." Is it our imagination, or does Noon growl "amen"? Naturally we would have preferred the bro to go Cracker vicious on Prof P's ass, having held his tongue on the subject for a whale's age. But: baby steps, baby steps. Springtime gets our Miss Jane up and moving though not fully returned to fighting weight, so it's a roly-poly daughter who piles out of the passenger seat into an armful of welcome. Since it's a Cracker bylaw that chubby trumps gaunt in "womenfolk," Mom and Dad are as pleased to see a thicker Jane as we were to overhear that "don't-think-I-like" verdict in transit. Back on the back-home farm, Miss Jane perks up. Crops get planted, Dad and bro manning the tractors, Miss Jane woman-ing the flatbed truck. In full-out doggy delirium, Noon rips-and-rares, ditch to woods to fields to ditch. Aunt Marveen stops by to brag about her latest gems-in-junk find. Mom puts her feet up for twelve seconds, watching the young'un she last saw rendered witless chase Noon round and round and round the yard, sit / stay be damned. No one but no one mentions Prof P; he's persona non grata for five stupendously care- and tantrum-free days. Hurrah / hurray!

Are we elated that our Miss Jane's feeling better, feeling vigorous, kicking up her heels? Absolument. Does our elation (also) mean we hope our Miss Jane will remain down on the (original) farm evermore? Hell no. Miss Jane is neither thirteen nor eighty. An old soul, perhaps, but an old soul currently residing in a (newly) twenty-three–year-old body. How can we, how can anyone in good conscience, wish her to stay snug where she started? Short answer: we can't. Nor should you. Nor should she.

23.

What happened to Seth B (i.e., Seth B's connection to our Miss Jane)? Have the two been meeting on the sly—say, in Christine W's empty apartment while Christine W auditions for *Cat on a Hot Tin Roof—The Musical*? Has Cinda G weighed in on the advantages of sleeping with friends (versus enemies) with a side lecture on the non-advisability of Sara Lee mope-fests? Has the bro, behind sis's back but on her behalf, reached out to Seth B with: "Talk to her, man! She'll listen to *you*."

Quite honestly we don't know where Seth B is, where he's been, what he's been doing or with whom. He's been scarce lately and via that scarceness, Lord bless, has refrained from: 1) hurling accusations, 2) demanding transformations, 3) behaving like a dick wagging a dick, 4) adding to the headache list of our Miss Jane.

You were counting on rescue by a knight-on-shining-motorcycle? Expecting the solution to Miss Jane's muck and mire to derive from the machinations of another MAN? Christ Almighty! Get with the program! Miss Jane and *only* Miss Jane must take the reins of Miss Jane. (Also, don't fret. We haven't seen the last of Seth B. He'll be at Miss Jane's party.)

24.

A party?

Miss Jane's throwing a *party*!?!

Whatever the extent of *your* surprise, imagine ours, her proclaimed trackers!

Did she dream up the bash on the drive back from the coast?

Confide in her bro?

Announce it as *done deal* to Prof P?

Beats us.

Day of, the hostess drinks her breakfast, lunch and dinner. Tippler Jane—another surprise. Wherever Prof P malingers, it's nowhere near the intoxication zone of Miss Jane whose intoxication levels, thus far, pose no delay / interference to party prep. She cooks, she cleans, she flower arranges. She lines the house with candles. She dusts the stereo, selects LPs. Throughout the day, Joni sings lead and Miss Jane sings backup, enthusiastically off-key. She goes to the store twice for ice, stocks the refrigerator with French onion dip. She bakes cookies. She bakes biscuits. She bakes banana bread. She sets out stacks of paper plates, towers of plastic glasses, bowls of pretzels, baskets of chips. She fills aluminum tubs with beer and soda, crowds counter tops with jug wine. She shampoos Noon, shampoos herself, dolls up in a maxi dress. She answers the phone, first ring, supplies directions to Buckhorn Road crisply and efficiently (i.e., nothing like a Cracker). As an extra guidepost, she ties red balloons to the mailbox and, in a tying fit, loops a bandanna around Noon's neck as well. She brushes her teeth. She combs her hair. She sits. She waits. She drinks.

Invitees? Just about every Tom, Dick and Harriet Miss Jane has crossed paths with since that short while ago (aka eternity) she entered a certain classroom, public university, South Atlantic region, invitations extended whether or not the invited classify as ally or adversary or continue to reside in the vicinity of Miss Jane's Ground Zero.

Final guest list:
- TA Alice
- Cinda G
- Seth B
- Prof K
- Carolyn Z
- Dorm Mother R
- A & E
- Joan C (!!)
- Therapist T
- Lovely Lynette
- Almost-as-lovely Kelly
- Kelly's Barry
- The Motel Pelican chambermaids
- Mildred E
- Margaret D
- Aunt Dottie
- Provost office (entire)
- The Tractor Trailer Training crew
- The psych tech (who fired the hostess)
- The Kelly Girl exec (who fired the hostess)
- The ear piercer (who maimed the hostess)
- Mel R
- Christine W
- Book groupies Tulane M / Susan J / Mary Y
- The bro (naturally)
- Prof P (unavoidably).

No-shows: everyone a decade older than Jane (with one exception), a subtraction that, in theory, ought to diminish the number of cars outside / bodies inside / septic tank strain but in practice somehow does not. The bro is MIA because, much as he loves his sis, he's no fan of madding crowds. Seth B is…detained. (Arguing with himself about whether or not to attend? Probably.) No neighbors to complain / call the sheriff, the loud gets very, very *piercing*—even for Noon, who heads for meadow repose. Prof P? Sensing dividends, he's pulled a switcheroo, bags Grumpy Fart for Party Dude. Presto / change-o, he couldn't care less about his cronies' boycott, surrounded by swirls of gals with whom he's yet the pleasure. Mary Y, Susan J—name any non-comatose female on-site and to her side Prof P sidles to forge a *deep*, *meaningful* connection amidst Frito Lay debris. When he steers toward Tulane M she performs a rolling tumble (to dissuade or further attract?), skips off to Miss Jane's porch, rifles Miss Jane's library and, under shelter of philodendron leaves, highlights all references to the consul's inebriated stroll, Day of the Dead. (Yeah, we can't get a true bead on Tulane M either.)

Our Miss Jane? Still drinking. Where? Beneath the kitchen table, encircled by legs of flesh and wood. From such an angle Miss Jane could glimpse, if looking, chips and dip smushed into the carpet, ice cubes dribbling, scorned banana bread kicked beneath the water heater, splashes of whatnot sticky-ing up the kitchen tiles. Could hear, if listening, the invitee of an invitee of an invitee shout to another: "Did that old guy just hit on you too?" When our Miss Jane crawls out of her self-imposed exile, we momentarily lose her in the mob, bob and churn. Another moment and we'd have missed the kitchen-door departure, the moon-doused figure crossing the yard, shadowed by a wagging tail and Seth B. We'd have missed altogether the vanishing Jane.

25.

Stars starring themselves. Ravenous mosquitoes. Damp, itchy grass. We won't pretend we aren't beginning to feel peevish, marooned in this endless night. We won't pretend we aren't edging toward *actively* resentful (aka deeply hurt), denied access to Miss Jane's current coordinates. We won't pretend the shutout isn't causing us to *critically* reevaluate our decision to take on The Cracker Hick / Chick Project in the first instance and, in the second, to *rigorously* question our continuing commitment to advocacy and espionage. The schedule? Punishing. The scope? Metastasizing. The finale? Indeterminate and potentially horrific.

What about *our* lives?

What about *our* bliss?

What about us, us, us?

Bums wet, backs achy, we are in sum wondering why we're *still* in the backyard of a Piedmont farmhouse, sun rising, waiting on our Miss Jane. And for that selfish, skanky, un-sisterly thought, the fairy godmother who's not supposed to be on the premises shoves the reason out the door, the better for us to observe Prof P in his boxers, swilling coffee and scratching his balls.

Okay.

Right.

Got it, FG.

Thanks for the reminder.

We won't forget again.

26.

Though unable to verify whether our Miss Jane a) *woke to find* herself *in a dark wood* or in the barn, b) glued to Seth B or at cautious remove, c) Noon her pillow or watchdog, we do know this: however Miss Jane spent last night and with whom, she emerges not our same Miss Jane. Repeating for emphasis: *Not The Same Jane.* One difference: she's carrying an armload of daffodils and dogwood. Another: she's alone. Noon is busy bidding farewell to Seth B down by the pond where, nine hours previous, Seth B parked to avoid the perpetration of drunken atrocities on his beloved motorcycle. Seth B's beloved Jane has other things to do.

Things?

What things?

Packing, actually—and not a weekend bag. House to car, trip after trip, Miss Jane drags, shoves, tugs and heaves: books, bags, baskets, plastics, shoes, socks, tampons, tea leaves, nightshirts, nightgowns, photos, seeds, Noon's bowl, Noon's leash, bro table, bro rocker, Joni LPs. How she'll stuff that whole kit and caboodle inside the station wagon, plus daffodil / dogwood posy, is a puzzle yet unsolved. Prof P's helpful contribution? Reality-not-sinking-in philippic delivered at a screech. *What does Miss Jane think she's doing? Where does Miss Jane think she's going? Does Miss Jane expect HIM to clean up HER party mess?* "Hadn't thought one way or the other," replies our gal without breaking stride.

OH—MY—GODDESS!!

Could we be prouder?

Careful to preserve Miss Jane's momentum, we pause but briefly here to address any lingering, laughable notion that Prof P truly cares for the female at whom he's screaming. Cross our hearts and hope to die: if Prof P had managed to find a Miss Jane sub, he'd be the one loading the car this early hour. But he hasn't managed to find a sub. May he never again. (Give it up, asshole! Retire the Henry Horndog Higgins shtick!)

Noon's already in the station wagon, voting with his rump. It's Prof P who's trotting back and forth, yipping at Miss Jane's heels. "In a year, you'll have no friends!" (Huh?) "You'll never be able to support yourself!" (Closer to truth.) "You made *me* more unhappy than I made you!" (Hmm. Even draw, we'd wager—*if* we were feeling charitable. But We're Not Feeling Charitable.) "You're ludicrous! Ridiculous! Second-rate! Third-tier!"—underachiever epithets that fail to slow the packing sequence.

Brava, Miss Jane! Brava! Keep up the pace!

Will Prof P body-block the station wagon? Fling himself onto the hood in protest? Cling to the elbow of a woman he deems mentally defective, not worth the tip of his pinkie? Nah. But he does throw his coffee cup at her windshield. (No worries. That's what wiper blades are for: wipe offs.) At driveway's end, Miss Jane turns left. At the next crossroads, left again, heading **west** versus her traditional east. Where's Miss Jane heading? We don't know and Miss Jane doesn't know either.

Please understand: this isn't / was never intended to be a once-lost / now-found saga, a late-20th century addition to the archive "Extraordinary Women of Their Time." Miss Jane's just a Cracker hick / chick low on cash, driving a seen-better-days vehicle, as yet unaware that not every landlord adores pets. Her life's work? Yet to be discovered. Who she deepest-down is / aims

155

to be? Ditto. Our on-the-road Jane is traveling blind in terms of destiny and won't arrive at that sweet spot on the space of this page.

The point, be it ever so humble: a woman needn't know the future to flee the present. Sometimes she just needs to

FLEE.

Celebrating:

—The escape of every Miss Jane;

—The defeat of every tiny tyrant.

Kat Meads is the author of six previous novels, two essay collections and several books of poetry and short fiction. Her plays have been produced in New York, Los Angeles and the Midwest. A native of North Carolina, she lives in California.